MY
CAMINO

MY CAMINO

PATRICK WARNER

A JOHN METCALF BOOK

BIBLIOASIS
WINDSOR, ONTARIO

Library and Archives Canada Cataloguing in Publication

Warner, Patrick, 1963–, author
My Camino / Patrick Warner.

Issued in print and electronic formats.
ISBN 978-1-77196-287-2 (softcover).—ISBN 978-1-77196-288-9 (ebook)

I. Title.

PS8595.A7756M93   2019   C813'.6   C2018-904454-3
                  C2018-904455-1

Edited by John Metcalf
Copy-edited by Emily Donaldson
Cover and text designed by Gordon Robertson

Canada Council   Conseil des Arts
for the Arts   du Canada

ONTARIO | ONTARIO
CREATES | CRÉATIF

ONTARIO ARTS COUNCIL
CONSEIL DES ARTS DE L'ONTARIO
an Ontario government agency
un organisme du gouvernement de l'Ontario

Published with the generous assistance of the Canada Council for the Arts, which last year invested $153 million to bring the arts to Canadians throughout the country, and the financial support of the Government of Canada. Biblioasis also acknowledges the support of the Ontario Arts Council (OAC), an agency of the Government of Ontario, which last year funded 1,709 individual artists and 1,078 organizations in 204 communities across Ontario, for a total of $52.1 million, and the contribution of the Government of Ontario through the Ontario Book Publishing Tax Credit and Ontario Creates.

PRINTED AND BOUND IN CANADA

CONTENTS

DUMBO

The Apostle John Sets the Scene

Let there be light, etc.

The art world oozed across the bridge into Brooklyn, pooling in the area now known as DUMBO (Down Under the Manhattan Bridge Overpass) to make a new centre of culture. A movement that would eventually spawn galleries and cafés, corporate offices in revitalized factories, real estate developments that capitalized on and even trumpeted the area's once-famous squalor. Photographs of brownstone low-rises crowded with immigrants, open sewers, street urchins sleeping on subway grates, all became part of the come-on: the black Moschino thong underneath the business suit, mystique with a tang of blood, the whole rags-to-riches creation myth fluffing the asking price.

You've seen the brochure, the one with the Brooklyn Bridge at the end of every elegant, tenement-lined street, the perspective and scale hinting tiny town, something doll's house and cozy in the heart of the heartless metropolis.

That's the place but not the place.

Our (not my) story begins before that time, on the night the bright star (IT) aligned for the very first time between the masts of the bridges, back when DUMBO was a no-go, a district of warehouses and potholed asphalt, deserted by all but predators and their victims.

IT appeared above our humble crib, bringing the tide that caused many boats to rise.

Into the manger entered a stranger.
Ask Jesus if God-the-Father's love is all-devouring?
Ask Joseph?
Ask the Virgin Mary?

Then He Peoples It

This is the story of Floss and Budsy and me, the Apostle John.

Floss and Budsy—not Beatrix Potter bunnies, but flesh and blood, man and woman, woman and man, and even a little something in between.

First He Budsy

Budsy: red-haired, white-skinned, weak-chinned, his sad face made distinctive by a too-long nose that turned savagely left at the tip, like someone had grabbed it and given it a god-awful twist. His sad face made memorable by eyes, blue-white as a malamute's, which he hid behind John Lennon shades.

Budsy: much given to silences, whom I met back in the day when I paid rent by driving a food truck between Manhattan construction projects, twelve-hour days shilling danishes (known in Copenhagen as Vienna bread), heroes, and Joe Timbuktu (heavily-salted) coffee.

Budsy, master electrician, reduced by rapacious recession to pulling wire through the walls of a midtown mansion. Genius child among tribal Mick carpenters, Guinea drywallers and decorators, none of whom loved him because he never wanted to reminisce about the old country (some rain-soaked bog town in County Despair) and because, after only two years in the new world, his accent had gone south before turning east for regions of the mid-Atlantic. Ambiguous identity is not much valued by guild members. Among new immigrants it's a cardinal sin—that is, until it matures across generations into something more venial, eventually revealing itself as the essential tool of assimilation.

Budsy: hell-bent on reinvention and devoid of iron filings that aligned with the geographically sentimental. Moody Budsy, whose smiles were always genuine, but whose habitual frame of mind was black cumulus and paranormal. There were days he would bend the fork of your thinking if you came within five feet of him.

Back in the days when we first met: every morning for six weeks, around 10—never before, always just after the foreman sounded his air horn—he appeared under the awning of my dented silver truck (Baby Bilbao with the opalescent hue) to buy a Fresca and a slice of walnut loaf, which he consumed barbarically—mouth like a trash compactor, spit-smacky sounds and crumbs avalanching into his lap—where he sat all alone on the stoop of that brownstone.

Then one day he stayed to talk.

No "hey, hello." No "wassup?"

High-minded Budsy. He wanted my take on the sculptures of Maurizio Cattelan. And why? He had spied with his little eye a copy of *Art Forum* on my dashboard.

Floss's Place

We said we'd meet at 6 at Floss's pad, 23rd Street.

It was the evening of the NIGHT of NIGHTS; the night the star (IT) came to settle and shine, twirl like the winning dropkicked goal between the uprights of the bridge, dull blue posts that absorbed both moonbeams and the lights of nearby Manhattan. It was the night when midnight drag-raced into the wee hours, when hard work conspired with luck to make the world roll over.

Floss had a walk-up just off 9th Avenue that smelled like vomit or microwaved buttered popcorn. Among the tenants were a mouse she called Meh and cock-a-roaches she referred to as Republicans. She would walk into her bathroom in the middle of the night and flip the switch just to watch them explode from some mysterious centre, tap-shoe in all directions across the Victorian tile, like Vera-Ellen in *White Christmas*.

Let there be light.

And there was.

Floss, Nostalgically

When she first made her move to the city, Floss began her day by sitting on the wide windowsill, knees up under her chin, coffee mug between her feet, a Marlboro Red making snap-crackle-pop noises whenever she took a drag. This was back in the day (years and years before the NIGHT of NIGHTS), when Floss was still the factory model; before she ditched her style (and much else) to become the art maven, the powerhouse, the icon of a community dispersed across continents.

She kept only two things from her old style: kohl-rimmed eyes, the outer corners finned: she was a Cadi. And her side-parted, nappy blonde curls, a near fro, hence her handle: Floss, since kindergarten or at least grade one.

Jar-always-half-full Floss, whose mouth, even when she was resting, bowed upward at the corners.

Her initial nine months in her first and only apartment in the city (for "first and only" read "rent control"—a Palestinian signed his sublet over before hightailing it to Boca Raton, his money made, to golf (therefore I am) and to drink (therefore I am not), that zero-sum game) five-foot Floss sat all the long hours of the day and night absorbing the city sounds: the throb and thrum punctuated by horn blare, tire screech, and brake squeal. The city's whale song took her deep into a spiritual ocean where everything was a shade of one shade.

Let there be a vault between the waters to separate water from water.

Life particles teemed all around her, invisible until the whole shoal turned, glittered silver for an instant, became the same shoal with a different shape. At such moments the hairs on the backs of her arms, on her neck and elsewhere stood up. This was electrifying—her being's essential spark touching the mother-lode—vision: self as substantively insubstantial, connected and disconnected, therefore mutable.

Here's what she thought: the future had sent a search beam to find her, lighting her up with a feeling of destiny. She was grateful. There was no need to broadcast the news. She would not cast her pearls before swine. She kept the memory safe inside her. This was her power source, her coppertop long-life lithium battery.

She was happy in her solitude until she was not. On such blue days, when turning into herself felt like turning against herself, she thought, "I am deluded," and reached for her bag of hippie lettuce. Soon the city's theremin was again singing its healing song. I am not one of them, she chanted. I can become anything I want to become.

She had left the nameless borough behind, barrel-bombed it. There was nothing but rubble: siding, brick, buckled wrought iron, shards of statuary, poisoned pressure-treated patio lumber and pesticide-soaked sod. So jagged was her break with the Irish-American tribe that she feared she would be the victim of an honour killing if she ever returned.

Disappearing into Manhattan was the easy part.

She took with her the cuckoo egg laid in her brain at birth—nay, long before (pre-his-stork-ic). That cuckoo's egg she came to see was not the work of an invader, a parasitic and opportunistic species, but her true nature, her perspective on it warped by the nest that society fashioned ten sizes too small for her. She nurtured it, allowed the oversized fledgling to hatch, let it turf out what in her was partisan; betray the dark and sentimental; out-ledger that fifth column.

Often she thought she had won only to suddenly smell the sulphurous fumes of Great Kills on her skin. The world's biggest landfill—visible from outer space—the frequent boast. It seemed there were things she could not *not* remember.

Some memories were just in her, like rebar. A truck shuddering to a stop below her window always placed her on the yellow ferry as it slammed into the dock at St. George.

But hard work paid dividends, in the end.

Hit send.

Twenty years on and the app of her new life was 95 percent loaded. She now thought of her early years only as markers to measure the distance she had come.

She measured it again that afternoon (the afternoon of the NIGHT of NIGHTS) as she listened to Budsy throw up in the bathroom, while they waited for me, the Apostle John, to ascend the stairs and knock three times.

That night, if all went well, if rumours proved true and promises were kept, she would pay off the mortgage on her new life. The seed she had planted would bear its first harvest: an apple to reinstate Eden.

The past would then be hermetically sealed.

Not that she believed this could happen—not in real life, no. But it would fuel the story, the mythology.

The Apostle John Arrives

Floss buzzed me up. "John, hon."

"Floss, bae."

Left-side mouth to right-side cheek and right-side mouth to left-side cheek. The left-side mouth to right-side cheek again. We were being very European. Foreshadowing, y'all.

"Ready for this?"

"I ain't never been more ready."

"Glass of Chablis?"

"You know me. Never say no unless I have to perform."

"No, then."

"Yes."

"Always the professional, J. Wish I could say the same for him. Says he's going to wear a ski mask. Doesn't want anyone to see his pasty mug."

"Last time he Warholed his hair and wore Jackie-O shades. Even his own momma wouldn't have recognized him."

"'Cept for the orange jumpsuit."

"Bespoke Guantanamo."

"Budsy brand."

From the tiny bathroom just off the galley kitchen came a noise like a plunger working a drain, followed by a slush sound, like congealed stew shaken from a stockpot and landing splat in a bucket. There came a groan, a kettledrum fart (bowl-amplified), more upchucking, and more flatulence; three farts this time, like suspenseful terminal punctuation. The toilet flushed. The sink taps splashed. Hands made a basin into which Budsy Donald-Ducked his face. The door latch flicked and out he strode; skin-tight orange overalls draining into green high-tops. Black ski mask with tiny eyeholes.

"That's offensive," I said, gesturing towards his headgear.

"Can and will," he said, walking over to the coffee table, where he picked up a bowling-pin shaped bottle of Riesling that was one-third full and downed it.

"At least eat something," Floss said.

Budsy walked into the galley kitchen and rummaged in the fridge, returning with a stick of old cheddar. Ate it like a Mars bar.

"The balaclava, Budsy, c'mon."

"The ski mask fucking stays or I do."

"Ok, dude. Just do us a favour and roll it up on your skull when we're outside. We don't want no NYPD on our asses. No

DHS motherfuckers capping you in the subway. Hell, those 5-ohs would probably take the opportunity to pop a few in *me*. I can hear them now: "Sorry, we missed." My ass shot thirty-five times. Not a scratch on you. I can see the headlines. Officers cleared of wrongdoing in accidental subway shooting. . ."

"You're nervous." Budsy said. "That makes me feel better."

"The balaclava, Budsy? I'm with John on this one."

"Ya. OK. I'll rim it 'til we get there. But the blinds come down once we're at the gallery. It's my new thing. Call me Mr. Incognito."

"Your choice, but you're going to suffer from the heat. Did I mention there'll be a hundred bottles of wine? And Gerry's on speed dial if we need more."

"What are we waiting for, so?"

*Abandon your towns and dwell among
the rocks, you who live in Moab.*

We walked to the 23rd Street station.

White pigeons—not your lice-ridden, gasoline-streaked, grey concrete chickens (these motherfuckers were more like doves)— strutted around the mouth of the cave, lifted off, fluttered hosannas all around us when a train pulled in and blew a warm blast of diesel air through that underground fallopian tuba.

We descended into the soot and filth, found the southbound platform, and waited.

The monochrome electronic Lite-Brite sign above the platform said *next train 1 min*.

I could already hear it rattling through the tunnel: kicked tin-can percussion underlying *Bitches Brew* brake squeak. Rocking grey metal face on the oncoming sawn-off train. An orange F like some badass school badge decalling the right-side window. Fat whitey driver at the kill switch on the left.

Thunder driving a piston of oily tropical air.

Carriages strobing to a stop.

Blanched faces looking somewhere between in and out.

Budsy on the platform almost apoplectic: rocking from heel to toe, his balaclava rolled to make a longshoreman's woollen knit, so cool above his chlorine John Lennon frames.

Floss had to nudge him—taser-finger his soft waist—to get him onboard.

Still, he waited for the whistle blast.

Inside, she took his hand and sat with him on the two-by-two seat, while I sat at ninety degrees to them in the pew of three.

The train was almost empty except for a street person who looked a lot like Saddam Hussein, not him of the dirt-stash and military uniform, but the late and beardy Saddam, freshly extracted from his culvert hidey-hole, having his teeth inspected.

Orange and yellow vinyl and wood-veneer partitions near the door. The floor an archipelago of blackened gum islands. A couple of sharpie tags on the wall—sweet cursive—the rest of the carriage corporate clean. Stainless-steel doors at either end, each with a window, like in a restaurant kitchen. As if waiters in tails carrying stainless-steel dome-topped trays would at any moment swan in, swallow through.

Floss's phone throbbed with incoming texts. She refused to look, fearing a torrent of last-minute regrets. Cunts.

To pass the time she lyric-gamed with Budsy.

"Who was first of the gang with a gun in his hand, the first to do time, the first of the gang to die?"

"Hector."

"And where did the stars shine?"

"On the reservoir."

"Word."

"And where did Hector watch the dawn rise?"

". . . Behind the home for the blind."

Floss beamed. "And we are the pretty, pretty what?"

"It's pretty, petty."

"No kidding. I always sang it pretty, pretty. OK. And we are the pretty, *petty* what?"

"Thieves."

"You got it. Where did Hector get a bullet?"

"In his gullet."

"And where did the poor lost lad end up?"

"Under the sod."

"Awesome. And now final Jeopardy: who did Hector steal from?"

"The rich and the poor and the not very rich and the very poor and he stole all hearts away."

Floss made it a duet. "He stole all hearts away. He stole all hearts away, away, away-a-hey. Away, away, away-a-hey. He stole all hearts a-way..."

Floss's strategy of appeasement and consolation gave Budsy the boo-boo he needed. Once more he climbed down from the catastrophere into the ordinary. One small step for humanity. One giant step for my Irish friend. It was a pilgrimage he made so often that by month's end his soul foot was known to bleed.

But now he was on the verge of a smile.

"Your turn," said Floss.

"More Morrissey?"

"Sure."

They knew I couldn't join in. Wouldn't even if I could. My head was a black hole for song lyrics unless the music was actually on. Even then I'd get it wrong. Songs I'd listened to a thousand times. Melody always trumped words, took me on a magical mystery tour through lands that didn't necessarily correspond with the word geography in the lyrics. I knew I was dealing with a true artist only when the songwriter and I ended up in the same location; bliss was to find myself in Lilliput, strapped down by some stranger's intention.

Floss, on the other hand, was a magnet for lyrics and tinny jingles. She could sing any commercial you could think of, and from as far back as you care to go. Cartoon themes, movie music, ad copy.

"*Plop, plop. Fizz, fizz. Oh what a relief it is.*"

Some of these had a Proustian effect on me.

"Alka-Seltzer!" I'd respond, on autopilot, surprised that the whole commercial culture was still in my head like some chronic infection. Those ad-man words a magic spell taking me back to my beige corduroy beanbag, from where I drank in cartoons on our old Phillips TV, a monstrosity with rabbit ears squatting in its cabinet, walnut finish with two dials and a panel of clunky buttons, the greenish screen and its perpetual pelt of static fur, the whole box on a lazy Susan base.

I could even remember what I was wearing: Mets sweatshirt, black-and-white tartan pants so tight in the crotch they inspired me to touch myself one quiet Thursday afternoon after school.

Now Budsy called and Floss responded, more Morrissey:

"Monday?"

"Humiliation."

"Tuesday?"

"Suffocation."

"Wednesday?"

"Condescension."

"Thursday"

"Is pathetic."

"By Friday"

"Life has killed me. By Friday life has killed me."

Budsy was rapidly sobering, his sometime better self superimposing on his loud shadow cabinet of selves, the pretenders knifing one another before falling on their own blades. He was getting real. This was a big night for all of us.

Grand Soir.

My nerves were afizz, like moonrocks. My thoughts pingponging between superlatives:

We were going to bomb / We were going to kill.

Budsy and Floss were in love / They hated each other.

They were a beautiful thing / They were a disaster.

How necessity was not only the motherfucker of invention but the vestibule of opportunity: how Budsy failed to get the arts grant he was sure his first review in the *NYT* had guaranteed. He couldn't make rent. Floss offered him her floor. Budsy said yes, and over the course of one purple-kush weekend, he levitated from carpet to couch to Floss's hard-packed futon.

I didn't see that coming, Floss said.

Neither did I. My BFF1 and my BFF2.

Some bitches pointed out that Budsy's sudden elevation into the Flossosphere coincided with the interest his installations were generating in the wider world. There are always people willing to throw shade, to dip torches in tar, to repurpose pitchforks. Still, it was undeniable—his last show had caused a social tingle that gave every indication it might soon intensify to a buzz.

York Street Station, Brooklyn

Steel wheels ground the rails as we pulled into York Street, York Street, York Street, York Street, York Street, the train depositing us at the far end of the platform. We shuffled upstairs, exited through the low art-deco doorway and walked south on Jay.

Jay Street Reminiscence

I was raw, just fourteen years old.

Instead of going to school one morning, I just stayed on the SIR and rode all the way to St. George, flipping the bird to Monsignor Farrell High and Mrs. Moltisanti as the train rattled past. OK, maybe I had half a plan as I climbed aboard at Huguenot, where I had spent the night at a friend's place. Call it a fluid idea that thickened as the train passed through Annadale, Eltingville, Great Kills, Bay Terrace, took on a cloudy hue at Oakwood Heights, where I should have hopped off, then began to solidify as we hit New Dorp, getting denser as we chugged up the line to St. George. I walked with hundreds into the terminal and waited to board a ferry that looked like a school bus grafted to a river boat.

I felt free.

On deck, I stood at the port-side rail, inhaled the diesel fumes and salt wash. Passing green, blind-eyed, torch-bearing statch, I gave the black power salute. Did the same again at Ellis Island.

Back on dry land, I took the R train uptown from South Ferry. No delays. No crazies. Just the early morning silence and the rise and fall, the sway and lurch of the rectangular metal boxes travelling through soot-shagged tunnels.

Before I could say Colonel Sanders, I was taking in some major art, basking before Basquiat at the MoMA. The most impressive thing about his work was the impressiveness conferred on it by the marmoreal surroundings. Scrawl in the palace of high culture. Some of the paintings looked like the dude took a pack of sharpies to a bathroom stall before using a reciprocating saw to cut a panel from the partition before framing and nailing it to the wall.

That jagged. That raw.

Which was cool, but it soon got tired. Yeah, I know what you're saying. The energy of the work. He was primal, an aboriginal original. Wild child. Haitian savant. Our brother, the other. And more such racist shit.

Thing was—least this was how I saw it—once he landed in the MoMA, he was bought and sold. Part of the machinery. Which I had a problem with and no problem with at the same time. Like, we all have ambition.

What really caught my eye that day was something more old-timey. Spied it when I stepped outside into the sculpture garden to smoke a Parliament.

Picasso's *She-Goat*.

A middle-aged security guard—spoke-one-word-at-a-time like he had some kind processing disorder—wanted to know why I wasn't in school.

Told me I was too young to be smoking.

Told me my momma and my daddy sure would be disappointed.

He was goading me, waiting for me to talk back so he would have an excuse to throw me out. I let him talk. Let his colour rise. Let the balloon under his starched shirt jiggle, push his key-shagged belt down another inch under his belly. He was a mosquito. I just kept staring at *She-Goat* until Uncle Tom faded.

That goat was one bad fatherfucker. Gave the lie to all that satanic shit. This was no devil. *She-Goat* didn't need no mythology. She roared with 1000ccs of goat power. She threw off some kind of steep sheep gravity. Anchored me to the earth and zuzzed at the same time, like a Jeff Koons steel balloon sculpture—all heavy and light. Like I was that sparkly diagnostic tool Doctor McCoy strobed over sick and injured redshirts on *Star Trek*.

Afterwards, I walked over to the park, piped a few crumbs of hash, and tried to understand what I had just seen. What did it mean? I'd gone to the river. I'd been washed in that water.

Still blissed-out two hours later, back on the train, looking at the *She-Goat* on a bookmark I picked up at the MoMA information desk, I forgot to change at Fulton Street. Before I knew it, I was in Brooklyn. Came up at Jay Street Station and walked into what looked like Nairobi or Freetown. Crowded street and everyone black. Mothers pushing buggies, most folks just ambling along; one or two pimp walks. No gangsters in sight but not a white face either.

Something like acid ate through my joy. It crackled in my ear like the ocean. Raw fear. I rode the first swell. Took hold and told myself to look again.

I was not about to be set upon.

I was not about to be killed.

No one was paying me any attention.

Everyone was just going about their business, cool as shit, like I was one of them.

Back on Jay in the Present Day

We hoofed it south until we reached a street of red-brick warehouses, where all three of us froze like we'd been bushwhacked simultaneously by the same hybrid and paralyzing thought that was equal parts savour the moment and equal parts wanting to turn tail on a dime and roadrunner it all the way back to the station.

Floss was suddenly all business. Brittle and honeyed, a sweet confection concealing fangs and claws. She stretched out her arms to the whole night and inhaled deeply through coke-furred pipes: "I'm getting tobacco, paint, beer, soap, and something else, cardboard and maybe pepper," as though able by scent alone to divine the history of the surrounding buildings.

Budsy loped ahead, before pulling a fast U-turn, his balaclava rolled down. "Motherfuckers move and I'll cap the pair of yiz, take you down, put yiz in a pine box six feet under, feed yiz to the worms that feed the fishes that will feed on your cement-sunk corpses should I change my mind and dump yiz both in the East River," he said in some kind of strange Mick accent.

He cartwheeled once, then twice. Upright again, he rested one foot on top of a fire hydrant and, leaning forward, said "Look, I'm Ziggy Stardust." His pimped-out nervous system had shifted gear from morose to antic.

Despite signs of gentrification, this was still not a street any brother would want to find himself alone on at night. Not like those Brooklyn streetscapes from the condo prospectus. The Manhattan developers had only just found a toehold.

Night crawlers, the current colourful crop of scab-encrusted meth-heads, devastated crack-hoes, and voluble hobo alcoholics were still present, though no longer abundant. Police patrols were frequently in evidence. Squats and shooting galleries had been padlocked and boarded over; reclamation and restructuring was well underway on many blocks. The down-and-out had little choice but to shuffle off to less green pastures. The remaining few who overlapped with gentrification would, at their deaths, be sanitized, immortalized on some street corner plaque, and, in some cases, sainted by the passage of time.

Time Is a Blip

What is it with time?

On the threshold of the NIGHT of NIGHTS, I loitered (without intent) with Budsy and Floss at the top of a street so long and straight that the parallel lines of warehouse walls on either side seemed to converge in the middle distance, like railway tracks at the gates to someplace unspeakable.

Nerves.

Low-voltage street lights staggered far apart. Shadows blackened potholes, made inkwells filled with a coma-inducing venom. I felt the globe flatten into two-dimensions, fold at the equator. A manhole cover flipped, popping into my hemisphere a South American Indian with a Cromwellian haircut, lip-plate, thong, and hunting bow. Without so much as a second thought, he dipped an arrow in a pothole and, aiming at my heart, let it fly.

The missile zipped past—I felt its draft—saw it strike a spark where the asphalt receded to reveal a layer of smeared brick cobblestones.

I lifted my eyes as if to the Lord: the smog-filled sky a soiled chamois buffing the stars invisible.

Whip It, Whip It Real Good

I was talking about time, how it flows like cream. How if you put it in the mind's bowl and turn on the mixmaster, it thickens. Experience and time whipped together have the appearance of something made to last.

Call it a memory.

But before that? A lot of confusion and extraneous detail that has to be repackaged and repurposed when the mind is more laid-back, chilled, more vacantly peaceful. Airiness must be beaten in. The ethereal (ideas and emotions) blended with the concrete.

On that night—the NIGHT of NIGHTS—the Floss Gallery was the bowl. One beater was art and one was expectation—I want to tell you about my installation.

But first I want you to picture the gallery: a glass-ceilinged foyer; a corridor with wide doorways opening into three rooms, two of them long and narrow and one as long but wider. The whole like the tines on a pastry fork—come on in and have a slice of the Big Apple art scene.

That night, Budsy's work was spread across two galleries, while mine was installed in the third, the smallest, the one visible through the front window. This was my consolation. It was Budsy's time. Not mine. I was there to lower expectation and make him shine (could be I'm overstating; thing was, I wouldn't have minded even if that were the case). My turn would come. He would do the same for me one day. Mutualism and all that.

Shit. Who was I kidding?

With this show, the Floss Gallery was out to amp the buzz that came from the *NYT*'s rave review (Sunday edition) of Budsy's recent Tribeca show. He was the standout from a group of five competition winners, the sore thumb, the awkward one who broke all the rules in just the right way—according to the critic who dedicated two of three one-inch paragraphs (printed in 8.7 point Imperial font) to Budsy's piece and only one paragraph to the other four. Soon after, dealers began to call on behalf of clients.

Floss immediately looked to capitalize, impose a Triple-A rating on the Budsy bond. A show was pulled together. Invitations were sent out. RSVPs received. The night was meant to be a mock coronation. It was billed in the community as Budsy's Big Break.

Neither Floss nor Budsy nor I nor anyone else really believed that the people who said they were coming would come. But their tweets re-tweeted and their Facebook "yesses" and "maybes" on a public page shared and re-shared would bring everyone else: the usual gang of artists, their friends, and coke-loving academics.

What I wasn't party to on the NIGHT of NIGHTS was the NEWS. What I didn't know was this: earlier that day, Floss got a text that made her face drain, made her pallid and damp as plain cream cheese. Whatever was in that message trampolined her into overdrive. I'm talking monster truck inside that tiny frame. Whatever was in that text—some mighty IT—lit up her genes like a string of Christmas lights; it was infectious, corrosive, contagious.

Floss: solicitous and encouraging to the new—especially the out-of-towners—and always ready to take the establishment down a notch or two. Too nimble of mind for those comfortable in their station and heaven help those poor schlubs who exhibited any sense of entitlement. The claws came out immediately: "Sure you'd help Jack on the horse. But would you help jack off the horse?"

Dopey Goldberg, long-time reviewer for the *Voice*, mouth opening and closing like a fish Floss had expertly jigged from the bowl, while everyone around him convulsed with laughter.

But I was going to tell you about my installation.

My first thought was that I would just rap, mix it up with a little beatbox. My beatboxing was, and is, righteous. I've paid rent doing it on the street, sometimes accompanied by my bucket-drummer, Harpo.

But my rap is another story.

Show, don't tell.

May as well.

The Apostle John Raps

In the beginning was the centre. And the centre was with God. And the centre was God.

Confused yet? This shit's hard.

How can my dog God *be* the centre and *be with* the centre at the same time?

Displaced once, twice, three times. A shell game.

The centre was beside itself all along, which explains why God was able to use sleight of hand to fool y'all into thinking the centre wasn't the centre no more.

The centre was Babylon before it was Rome.

The centre *was and is* a mighty big word and if you can't spell it you a mighty big fool.

The centre was and is IT. And that's no acronym. No trap.

You need to be an acrobat to keep up with my rap.

IT don't stand for information technology—keep your over-caffeinated, Facebook-distracted, Twitter-pated, smart-phone-tweaking mind on the flow, bitch.

IT *was and is* it, with a capital I and a capital T. As in ITch.

IT *was and is* the power, the control, the space into which all other places, persons, and things wanted to flow.

IT be the person trapped in a noun.

IT be the place defined in a noun.

IT be the thing locked in a noun.

IT be the noun wantin' to verb.

IT be the business. The herb.

IT couldn't change biology—though it never stopped trying—and by biology I mean the by and bye, mortality, the door-stop of doorstops, big D, I mean death.

IT *was and is* life. The Centre. My breath.

IT was Style. It changed.

IT ebbed and flowed. But it remained constant. It remained.

IT multiplied and remade itself as satellites—some of them so strong that people couldn't tell them from the real thing.

IT pretended to reside in one person (the man), but IT knows the centre *was and is* no island. IT could make any place sing.

IT could fight wars and it did—gore fests, rape ruts, genocide conventions, disease decathlons, suicide convocations, starvation conclaves, shit that had to be seen to be believed—but the first half of the twentieth century taught IT the error of its ways.

IT knew the centre could no longer hold.

Anarchy be stomping his boots on the world.

No choice but to fight fire with fire.

IT survived by pointing a snub-nosed *Little Boy* at its very own brain. Like that crazy sheriff in *Blazing Saddles*. Held his own self hostage.

IT was going to stop playing God by playing God. It would manage.

IT would prosecute, prostitute, and proselytize a new philosophy. It would move to the periphery and all places in-between. Every place would have permission. Everyone would be empowered. The world was decentred.

IT became *it*.

THE became *an*.

Light would shine into the darkness and darkness would not overcome it.

Battle, y'all.

My Rap Don't Flow. My Rap Don't Rhyme.

My Rap's not hip. Never was. Truth is, it always stunk. Rang in my head—even when I was deep in the flow—like a subway token in a handful of coin. Like that bit above—I called it "Decentre."

Too nerdy. Too brain-a-tonic.

My rap's bubonic.

You had to read books to dig my rap.

Your neurons had to be firing.

My rhymes were internal.

Not that infernal end rhyme.

Though I use it sometimes.

My heroes were Gil Scott Heron, Dream Warriors, Digable Planets, and The Fugees. I came late to the game. By the time I got in, jazz had gone out. It was all gangsta. Bitches and hoes. Mares eat oats and does eat money and Lil' Kim eats ivy.

Sad thing is, I liked to battle. Had no problem taking my shit uptown or over the bridge to Brownsville or Coney. I'm not afraid of anyone, can outtalk the lippiest motherfuckers. But those brothers shot me down every time. Never won a single battle. No, sir. Not one.

They said I had no flow. My beats broke the bar. My syllables were too irregular. My rhymes broke lines.

What worked in a Soho loft or in the dorms of NYU bombed in freestyle. Brothers told me I had something but it wasn't street. It belonged on the page.

And what colour is the page?

That's right—it's what they wouldn't say.

Whiter than white. I rapped like a white boy.

This was the subtext.

I wasn't black enough.

Don't believe all the business about community and inclusiveness and the rainbow coalition. Rap community be the most conservative on the planet.

So I tried poetry slams.

I tried writing my shit down and sending it out to magazines.

Used to rhyme about the reject letters and the ivy-league editors who thought they knew better.

White folks kept asking me about my influences: had I read Langston, Countee, Maya, Nikki, and World Wide Du Bois?

The subtext being, I was too black.

The only place my shit seemed to work was with the art crowd. Where they read it as parody, as anti-rap, where my in-between status was considered an asset.

So I hooked up with Budsy and Floss. They told me—hell, convinced me—I had a gift for performance. Spoken word.
First time at the Floss Gallery, I beatboxed with a gilded turd.
It went over big.
It was a hit.
I was the shit.
I'm finally getting to my installation.
My most minimal minimalist creation.
One word.
Word.

The Apostle John's Installation, a Further Hint

It was site-specific. That's how it is with all performance art and many—"Say me say Many Moni, say me say manymanymany"—art installations. They work only in-situ; they are an immovable constellation. Makes them the little piggies that rarely make it to market.

To understand how my installation worked, you'll have to picture the view from the street in through the main gallery window. On the windowsill is a row of shot glasses, each containing three cigarettes: nicotine stalks with imaginary smoke flowers.

People were standing around outside. The sidewalk congregation was a mixture of hipsters: guys in plaid shirts, skinny jeans, and sporting Yosemite Sam beards. Girls in retro dresses—structured, textured, patterned—and army boots. They accessorized with horn-rimmed glasses, strings of pearls, or knitting needles in muss-piled buns. Or, they wore the same threads as the guys, but with buzz-cut hair, short back and sides, like Cold War flying aces.

Scattered among them were the middle aged, the droop-titted in shapeless-but-expensive black clothes, accented with artisanal scarves, wraps, or ponchos; and with them their men, the grizzled and paunched, in stretch jeans and leather jackets.

The area just outside the window was an aviary, loud with chatter.

Overheard

From a beardy know-it-all. Fucking verbatim: "Queer culture gravitates towards the art world. Folks of the LGBTQ community have a deep investment in inventing their role in society. Add to that the shock value and boundary erasure that is so much a part of any art scene in any age. In this environment, even straights come across as camp. The image of the artist as testosterone-driven, hard-drinking cattle driver may be meant as a corrective but it comes across more as male burlesque."

The Solitaries

Representing their private "isms" outside the Floss Gallery that night were the solitaries (all of them whispering quiet Our Fathers and Hail Marys).

Dudes in black threads: "I'm waiting for a friend to show."

"I'm waiting for a date."

Young artists in their first winter. A bowl of spicy bar nuts with a few bland grad students thrown in.

They smoked.

They tapped phones for Snapchat and Instagram.

They tried to look like they didn't give a damn.

They studied the ground as if for inspiration: the half-exposed cobbles flecked with cigarette butts. Maybe one cork-papered filter bore the imprint in red lipstick, the little lines where puckered lips perfectly impressed, a small intimacy implanting itself like a seed in the artistic imagination and resurfacing in future work. Some *Great American Nude*, dude.

Mostly they gazed inward, a focus that, looking in through the gallery window, only intensified.

Reflect on this scene a minute; wrap your head around and through it. Let that gauze-enclosed thought steep in the brown betty of your skull. What is a gallery but the external manifestation of the artist's internal theatre? Where better for artists to confront themselves and their dreams?

The space visible through that showroom window was the smallest of the three rooms: more like a galley than a gallery. Hanging on the facing wall was a mirror, a big motherfucker, about the same shape as the window but smaller and with its vertical sides leaning over to the right, like that geometrical shape—what's it called? a rhombus, yeah, that's it. Gave you the idea that the mirror was actually the shadow of the window, but cast at an acute angle from a light source somewhere behind and to the left of where the viewer stood. Clear as mud?

Sooner or later, you just know a solitary is going to walk up to that window and look inside. Hand shielding his eyes to cut the glare, block out the background reflection. And what is he going to see?

Only his own sad-sack face looking in.

A kid gazing into a candy store. Cliché.

He *was and is* locked out.

He can no longer see the people standing around him.

He can hear them, smell them, even feel their heat, but he can't see them.

He is set apart both from the world he is in and the world he wants to enter.

Poor little Greenie.

And the effect is intensified by the window frame: heavy, ornate, and covered in what looks like gold leaf, like the big gilt motherfucker framing on early modern works of art; only in this case the gilding wasn't gold leaf at all but cigarette foil.

Dig it?

Get what I'm saying?

The Gilded Frame

Story was that Floss placed a classified ad in local newspapers asking smokers to send in their empty cigarette boxes. From these she removed the papers, separating silver from gold. The liberated golds she then brushed with egg and applied to the frame before burnishing the whole rectangle with a dog's tooth.

Real postmodern.

And real clever, too, because it intensified the space. You stood outside and stared past your plate-glass reflection through the window and caught, there on the inside, an image of yourself. The frame made it feel to anyone looking in as if they were looking at a painting in which they themselves were the subject.

The chosen ones.

Entering the Floss Gallery

Walk with me now down the alleyway, past the plywood wall plaque, the Floss Gallery inscribed by Budsy with a kid's *Burn Rite* iron.

Alley walls painted matte black, the brick cobblestones an upchuck yellow. Nature's hazard-warning colours meet the road to Oz. A Beatles mixed message, like when McCartney chirps "It's getting better all the time" while Lennon sneers "It can't get no worse."

The whole yin and yang thing.

The bitter and the sweet.

At the end of the alley, two spotlit steel doors on which someone has scratched a heart, bisected with an arrow, and scored
with R.S. and V.I.P.

Only Floss knew if those initials meant anything to anyone.

Herring-Do

Facing us when we entered the foyer was an oak podium, the kind
maître d's stood behind in fancy restaurants. A body couldn't help
but look around for the monkey suit.

Turned out the podium was a plinth.

It had a bronzed and burnished object mounted aslant—
microphone-style—on its top. A glance scoped that object as having one of nature's primal, final, and most recognizable shapes.

Not a mic.

Not an ice-cream cone either.

It repelled and attracted.

Knobby-lumpy was thick at one end, then tapered gracefully
to a slender tip. The whole spoor about eight inches long.

That's right. I'm talking turd.

Bronzed and shellacked, with a small title card that read sim-
ply, "Herring-Do."

I'm serious.

Say what you like about it, it caught your eye. It had shock
value. It served notice to visitors that what they were about to see
in the galleries might get up in their grills.

It was into that mic-mimicking object that I rapped the night
the gallery opened, a little under two years earlier.

Shit. Time again. Go fast/go slow. It will all be over before you
know it.

On the Floss Gallery's opening night everyone wanted to know
the name of the Herring-Do artist. Floss put out that it was none

other than the Singaporean Ai PuhPuh. Only me and Budsy knew the truth: the work was produced at the end of a long and decadent fish banquet. The artist returning from the bathroom, holding a shoe box, and announcing she had at last achieved something close to perfection.

Oh, that *anonymiss.*

Poly Centric

Arranged in a crescent, a group of crazy-looking women guarded the gallery entrance. Try to push through and they moved with you.

A rubber band.

This freaked some folks, especially the uptown types who came later. There was huffing and puffing. I overheard several "would you minds" (yo, out of my way), and "well, I nevers" (what the fuck, bro). One turbaned woman totally lost it and started rooting through her Louis Vuitton bag, extracting from it a bottle of prescription medication.

You could say that people were just slow, but art can be so many things these days that it's often hard to tell just what it is that shimmers before your eyes. Is that paint-shagged denim jacket draped on the wooden stepladder an exhibit, or was it left behind by the man who touched-up the gallery walls?

But most people got it right away.

The door gals were a roaming installation.

Floss's idea.

This was Poly Centric and her peeps: Sasha, Martha, Jill, and Marcella.

Sibyl-like, Poly stood facing those trying to enter the gallery, her orange dreads hay-stacked, her curvaceous body swaddled in a white sheet. She wore what looked to be welders' glasses with opaque lenses. When anyone approached, the whole group closed in around them. Poly thrust out her right arm, palm up, gesturing stop. The lenses of her glasses turned clear, revealing mad eyes. No one spoke. Ten, twenty, thirty seconds passed. The tension grew until Poly's glasses snapped pale again and the group parted to let the visitor through.

Floss told me later that people had complained, found the experience "too invasive." She rolled her eyes when she said this.

Floss Bill Clintons and Budsy Bob Doles

Ruffled, unnerved, expectant, the guests made their way into the galleries.

Floss greeted them with all the warmth of a woman encountering a long-lost, much-loved sibling. She made each person feel like the centre of the world.

Meanwhile, Bob Doling it near the bar was Budsy, his balaclava pulled down, the wool around his mouth flecked with droplets of white wine and condensed breath.

The excitement was building.

Time was beginning to carousel.

Conversation assaulted from all sides as I made my way through the crowd. "Ya, oui, Tom Wolfe, he called zeh contemporary art world the *statusphere*."

Belgian, Swiss, and Parisian accents. Rumour had it that these Europeans were a movable installation. Rent-a-Wreck sophistication, a diversion from the business of art, the horse trading.

Floss Advises

Floss was in earshot, bending the tempeh-coloured ears (if skin tone was any indication) of a couple of vegans.

"Painting may be out, hon, but it's always going to be easier to sell. So if you want your canvasses to find buyers, don't use brown. It's too much of a downer. Use more reds, blues, and greens. It makes sense, right? No one wants a gloomy painting. I mean if you have to look at it every day. Makes sense, right?

Also, as much as you and I might like looking at nude men, you have to be aware of the prejudice. That's what I'm saying. If you want your painting to sell, make it a babe with nice boobs and a bodacious booty, in some classical pose, nothing too sexual, unless it's for the bedroom, but even then you have to tread carefully. No woman wants to feel second rate in the privacy of her own home.

So ya. Painting may not be considered cutting-edge anymore, but there's still a market.

Don't expect to have an easy time selling stuff that has to be plugged in or that needs a whole room of its own or a team of technicians to assemble it.

And last, but not least. And this may sound really dumb, but it's a fact. Don't make your paintings too big. They have to be able to fit through a standard door or be carried up a stairwell. And they can't be too long either. They have to be able to fit in an elevator. I'm serious.

Most big city collectors live in apartments. They want something they can bring home and hang on the wall. That's the world we live in. So that's my advice if you want to sell to private collectors. That's the business."

Gallery A: Budsy's Panic

Panic consisted of seven framed images. Each was a life-sized photograph of a chest x-ray but Renaissance-filtered to make the surface look like crackled paint. The works were mounted on bright white walls and lit from overhead with brilliant LED lights.

The medical subject matter had viewers hunting for abnormalities: a tumour, a radish vein, or some other distortion. Why would anyone bother to present a healthy set of lungs? A pulmonologist would have known at a glance that this was exactly what they were—a perfectly normal pair of lungs—and would have beat it out of there. And so she would have missed the point.

Budsy was always looking to demonstrate that the educated eye was as blind in its own way as the untrained eye. Just a different set of biases, y'all.

Only those who stayed to contemplate his pictures were let in on the mystery.

The first painting was gently breathing, the surface growing slightly convex before flattening out, the rectangular frame waxing a miniscule amount towards the oval before resuming its right angled-ness.

Each subsequent painting in the series added another dimension: a slight wheeze—not that it could be heard above the background hubbub—or the frame slowly changing colour, from oxygenated pink to pallid.

The effects grew more obvious as viewers made their way along the gallery.

And just in case anyone missed the joke, the last picture in the sequence took to shuddering at twenty-minute intervals, a fit that culminated in the frame popping its hinges and falling to the floor.

This was not particularly popular with the gallery staff.

The seven works were for sale only as a set.

The Apostle John's Installation, at Last

Angelo, once the Lionel Messi of movie critics, now of *Artforum* fame, was there, idling at the back of Gallery C, observing a group corralled on the red carpet. One said:

"There's nothing to see."

"I saw something."

"Is this a joke?"

"No. Really. Over there."

The carpet was narrow; two could not pass abreast without one turning sideways.

Angelo watched. The initiated knew to approach him from the left only. He would not respond to anyone who approached him from the right. This had been going on for several years. Was it a political statement? Did he suffer from a chronic ear infection? Was it tinnitus? Some said he had gone deaf in one ear—the result of a right hook from Mickey Rourke, an assault written up in the *NYT*—and he was just too vain to wear a hearing aid. His close friends, his posse—made up of one other critic and those artists he championed—knew it was all about control. It was about exclusion and insider knowledge. He was a kingmaker. It was a creative statement. No one in the art world—not even Angelo—was unaffected or unselfconscious.

"There! I saw it over there."

"Saw what? I was looking that way."

The roped-off red carpet ran about a third of the way into the room, to just about where the window began. Blank white wall to the right, with a leaning mirror reflecting the window on the opposite side of the room. Blank white wall straight ahead, but spotlit. This was a decoy, as was the mirror that reflected the window. People pondered the spotlit absence; then puzzled over the mirror reflecting the street, where the hoi polloi gazed in on the gallery space.

"I saw it again. Over there this time."

"Where? Goddamn it."

The woman was referring to one of seven small screens embedded in the walls, which were constantly flashing the word *Chosen* for intervals of 250 microseconds, making them undetectable to the conscious mind. At other random intervals, the screens flashed the word for 500 microseconds, making the word detectable only to some people.

My idea was to have folks leave the installation frustrated, aware of what they were supposed to see but not having succeeded in seeing it, despite their best efforts.

Secret handshake.

No fairs.

Old Girls' Club.

You get the picture.

Among those who claimed to have seen it, some would be liars.

You know who you are.

Angelo, leaning against the back wall, gave me a smile and an approving nod. My whole body lit up, zuzzed like a near-end-of-life fluorescent bulb. I pulsed. I tingled. My hair stood up as if brushed with static. I could picture the write-up in *Artforum*. *Artforum!* My inner little bitch was jumping up and down, shaking her pigtails, clapping her littlse hands. This was going to be major.

And it would have been
had the night
not received
an unexpected
visitor.

MiCS

Four white folks standing in the foyer were my first clue that some extraordinary shit was about to go down. The women—I kid you not—in furs and evening gowns. Their shoes—their shoes, like nests excreted by some kind of tropical insect. The men in Armani or Hugo Boss. Their watches, which they checked every few minutes, were like underwater explosive devices. *Ocean's Eleven* shit. They were on their way to somewhere else, I thought, a reception with the mayor at the NYPL. A dinner party on the Upper East Side. A fundraiser for republican puppet theatre. Yeah, I'm talking *those* kind of people. The men silver-haired, age-spotted, saggy-buff. The women botox-taut and moisturized. Barracudas gliding grinningly. Poly Centric and her crew didn't even try out their shtick. They just open-sesame-ed and let the rich fish swim on by. Two more limousines pulled up outside. More furs. More dresses. Fragrances squeezed from the glands of albino civet cats. Paxil-composed temperaments.

The buzz in the gallery scaled electric as the regulars registered the sea change. Both shaken and stirred, those already inside decided to up their game. Downtown would not be cowed by uptown. Floss homed in on the moneyed set, a buzzard on fresh roadkill. Budsy stood behind her, his mouth showing pink through the hole in his black mask.

And then suddenly there *he* was. The man I would never have expected in a million years. Shit. Here was, without a doubt, the sender of the vampire text that had drained Floss's face earlier that day. The God Man. All seven lank feet of him, in his trademark cream suit with the green satin lining and the tangerine buttons. MiCS (Man in Cream Suit) as he was known internationally. The boy from Hell's Kitchen. Son of a city transit worker. Irish American. Untrained. Unschooled. The man with the eye. The über-dealer who competed with museums. The single most powerful geezer in the art world. He was smoking a long pink cigarette. Who was going to stop him? And he was talking. That distinctive voice: a flutter of sibilance and lisped S's: a susurration. Poplar trees in a gentle breeze. And with him, listening as though his career depended on it—none other than Ed Ruscha.

MiCS Speaks (Detonator)

"Think of the art world as hub with six spokes:
    artist,
    dealer,

curator,
critic,
collector,
and auctioneer.

"The rim of this wheel makes a complex trail in history and even in prehistory. The dull-witted see it as a series of tracks leading directly from the past to the present. Such people believe in progress, in mankind as perfectible. Which is a species of scientific thinking. We indulge it because it feeds the art market and its current insatiable need for the contemporary. The artist and the critic know, however, that the genius of Lascaux has not been improved upon. Only restated, embroidered, if you like, in the millennia since its creation. The artist knows that the tracks crisscross, turn back, come to dead ends. She wanders this labyrinth chased by the minotaur of her own talent. The critic knows that it is merely a puzzle, and, with characteristic hauteur, likens it to the kind of maze you find in the back of a children's comic book. He attempts to trace it with a pencil. He, too, wanders, chased by the minotaur of his theory. There are maps, of course. Pollock drew many of them, for those with eyes to see. As have you, my friend. As you have, no doubt, in your best work. Long after art is dead and the human has been pharmaceutically, genetically, and robotically enhanced, neuroscience will return to art and literature to rediscover the original brain."

The Moment of Truth

Floss approached MiCS, arms outstretched, as for crucifixion.

MiCS, leaning in, kissed her, once, twice, three times. He stared into her face, his expression one of cosmic amazement embroidered on something hard and inscrutable.

Floss changed colours like a hooked and dying dorado fish. Like she knew this was it. This was death. The presence of MiCS in her gallery—no matter what the outcome—meant death, the end of her old life. The collapse of a star.

I couldn't hear what they talked about. I couldn't get close enough. Artists and hipsters—the young donkeys—crowded around, pretending not to listen as Floss shepherded MiCS into the main gallery. Budsy walked next to them (balaclava still rolled down—gotta hand it to you for that, Buds, man), drunk and trying to be solicitous, looking like some punk-ass butler.

Floss led MiCS to the door of the gallery where Budsy's main work was installed and gestured that he should go on ahead, alone. MiCS stopped as if to take inventory or to savour the moment: a private viewing in a crowded gallery. All that was missing was a blast from the brass section and someone to run in from the wings and drape an ermine-fringed cape over his shoulders, hand him a scepter.

He entered between two spans of white wall: no pictures. He walked forward. Inset at the back of the room was a vast basalt-black mirror, its surface less polished-looking than wet. He walked toward it slowly, saw himself reflected. Behind him, the bright entrance to the tomb-like space was stacked with the heads of all those looking in.

The hubbub, the chatter followed him but now it held a false note, as though people were talking just to make it seem like they weren't watching him.

He moved forward.

Stopped.

Something was wrong. He was suddenly not there.

He walked closer. The mirror had made a fundamental error, capturing everything in the room but him.

MiCS was on it—clearly it was some kind of projection ... the surface no longer reflective, was a screen.

His next thought was that he was being watched—not by those at the doorway but by a secret gallery. He registered the effect. A clever trick.

This was how he felt whenever he stood before a great work of art. He felt read by it, judged by it. The dead had come to watch the watcher bungee on a length of his own intestine.

He contemplated his response: he could Fosse it up with a ballsy show of brio, put a stop to their gallop with his Irish gene, Gene Kelly it across the parquet, cop a plié, let them know (nudge-wink) he was in on the fun, let them have it right in the Blahniks.

Or he could be humble. He could react as though this really was a great work of art.

It was a business decision.

Gingerly, he approached the image of the room, the screen still behaving as though it were a censoring mirror. He stopped an arm's length from it, planting his feet as directed, firmly on two blue footprints.

He leaned forward.

A woman's face appeared where his should have been. Her grey-white skin was wet and luminous. "What do you see?" she asked, her wavering smoky voice pure Eartha Kitt kitty-cat coquette.

The rest of her body appeared.

He stared coolly at the moving image, took in the sharp cut of her mini-skirted leopard-print suit; that urn of light between her slack thighs; shirt pleats that foamed up into ruffles; her hair in an asymmetrical blunt cut, like a wig askew; her nose no nose at all, but two shadow holes, the kind that hammer blows emboss on the annals of drywall; pupils black as the screen that contained her; plump lips pursed while she crooked a finger, hennaed up to the second knuckle, motioning him to come closer.

Her whisper phlegm-flecked, streptococcal.

She spoke in clicks that pulled a trigger that tripped a neon sign on the wall.

A phrase in cursive lit up behind her, behind him: the words *reveal/conceal*, conceal/reveal, alternating in flashing amber.

Perfect, he thought. Right up to the flashing sign. That's a bit over the top. It's a bit cheap. But easily fixed.

The Man in the Cream Suit turned around, made solid eye contact with Floss, and then, with a nod to Budsy, he began to clap.

A Great Hokusai

His applause announced a coming tsunami, a great Hokusai wave arriving from the farthest points of the globe, gathering anger as it crossed the seven oceans, converging on Brooklyn from Jamaica Bay, from Upper Bay, from the Hudson and East rivers to come crashing through the doors of the Floss Gallery at 11:42 that night.

At 11:32, everything remained tentative. The party had not yet shed its skin. People were still nervous, either too unsure of themselves to let it all hang out, or overcompensating and letting too much of it hang out. Making fools of themselves.

Next thing—figuratively speaking—John Belushi walked in with the tequila. Shot glasses—three rows of ten—were lined up on the counter. Salt got licked. Elbows got bent. Lemon got sucked.

And just like that I was gone. Like King Louis in the *Jungle Book*. Solid gone.

It was twelve hours before I clocked in again.

By then, I was back in Floss's crib, sunk in the crumb crevasse between the cushions and the back of the couch. Budsy was passed out on the futon. Someone was cocooned inside a sleeping bag on the floor. Floss was in the bathroom gargling some Billy Joel song I couldn't name even though I'd heard it a hundred times. I had a hangover of Old Testament proportions. But pain and nausea were mown down by the ibuprofen of endorphins still lingering from the night before—which began with MiCS applauding, a signal for everyone in the gallery to do the same.

The Apostle John Recalls

Floss linked Budsy with one arm and MiCS with the other, and led them through *Panic* and afterwards down to Gallery C, to see my work.

I was all tongue-tied.

MiCS was not what I expected. The dude was humble. I remember him saying this: "People like to talk about themselves. They like to show off their learning. I am fighting that urge right now—I have to fight the impulse to try to impress you that I am important. What is important is your work. Budsy's work. What Floss has accomplished here."

The young donkeys kept crowding around him.

I went to do a line with Budsy in the back room. When we came out, MiCS was gone.

"Don't worry," Floss said. "Gary has gone for more wine."

2:00 a.m. and the clink of empties being loaded into garbage bags. We stacked plastic glasses into spines and competed to see who could carry the tallest one to the dumpster without tipping it.

Then Floss was in my face saying, "Please say you are OK. Please say you're OK."

"I'm OK. Why?"

"Cuz MiCS just texted and invited us to a party in the Bowery."

The Bowery Loft

White brick walls, white wood floor, industrial ceiling, zinc conduits. Three black, semi-circular couches in a sunken circular pit. MiCS sitting across from James Franco and Harvey Keitel. Other rich and famous folks there, too.

I remember a lot of vague talk about art and a lot of specific talk about business.

I found that weird but I let it pass.

Which means I couldn't have been that drunk.

"The best thing an artist can do to increase the value of her art is to die. Finitude equals market definition, equals mark-up. The best thing a collector can do when his stock goes into decline is buy more of the same, deliberately overbid in order to keep prices high for certain artists.

"I'm here to tell you that the fusty-musty antiquarian art world of the past is no more. The art market of today is a mall. People want the new. It's retail, darling, not previously loved.

"I never read anything about art. I look at the pictures and let my guts decide. Which doesn't make things easier. My best discoveries cause me the most severe gastric distress. At the same time, it's sexual.

"People think art is too expensive, that we are in a bubble. And yes, I can't disagree, even though the art market is bigger now than it has ever been. There are probably only about 7.3 million people living today who would pay to see it or own it. But what you have to remember is: that number will be sustained and may even grow—more and more people are educated and visual culture is quickly replacing literary culture—so you are betting on the future. The current price is an indicator of the number of people in the future who will experience the piece. This is the reason the current market seems bloated. In fact, it is not."

What It All Meant

There were no kneelers and no pews; there was no high altar, no incense, tabernacle, or perpetual light. There was no distinction between worshipper and priest. But like it or not, this was a church. And everyone in it that night was a believer.

Conceptual art. Art of all sorts.

It gave us meaning, a sense of purpose.

It was a community.

Which wasn't to say that it didn't have its prophets, who at various times appeared sainted, who broadcast our existence to the wider world. Sometimes a person got so branded that other people began to use terms of divinity.

But it was all local, of course. Even if it was global. To be inside it was to know this. In the same way that Jesus remained unknown in the wider world while he was alive, while those around him recognized his weight, his coming world-title bout. So it was with MiCS, whose presence in the life of an artist moved her up several classes.

So it was that night when he entered the Floss Gallery.

Into the manger entered a stranger.

Ask Jesus if God the Father's love is all-devouring?

Ask Joseph and the Virgin Mary?

MiCS's taste had become the lens through which the whole art world poured and reflected back upon itself. News would soon spread about Floss and the artists she represented. And it did. Before it ever hit print or even digital, tongues foretold that MiCS was going to remount that night's show at his flagship gallery in Chelsea.

And if *that* was a success, he was going to take it to London.

Which meant that everyone present in the Floss Gallery for the original show started projecting themselves into the future, where they would find the importance of this night (and the part they played in it) confirmed.

This was where the rubber met the road.

This was the moment.

Art was shucking its skin.

The illusion of a cutting-edge shattered and, for a second, everyone saw that what for some time had been passing as original was nothing more than mechanical reproduction, variations on overworked themes, art that had the appearance of Art. Conservatism had crept in. Entropy was in play.

MiCS's presence confirmed that Budsy and I had taken real risks, that something unique was happening at the Floss Gallery and that it was about to be rewarded.

Not that it was always clear just what or who was being elevated—as one of the principal artists exhibiting that night, I thought my little boat would rise on the same wave; I expected prices to jump 50 percent by Tuesday; I expected the light on my voicemail to blink dementedly. How wrong I was I would not find out until much later.

So not only the artists there that night, but the dealers, curators, and buyers also felt the magic touch. They were there first. If they adapted their own style and taste accordingly, they might be seen in retrospect as being in the vanguard of the new wave. Vaunted early-adopters.

Not even the critics were immune.

Angelo, of *Artforum*, immediately responding to the magnetic change, began to reply only to those who spoke into his right ear.

Little did we—the artists—know that we had just become the subject of a hostile takeover.

CAMINO

Prologue: Part I

Bae Floss was a hectic, run-around bee in the thirteen months following the NIGHT of NIGHTS, the night of the great Hokusai and Budsy's febrile ascension.

She was travelling with the mighty MiCS to biennales around the globe, or lunching on blowfish and shark at his offices,

or swapping palm sweat with Eurotrash dealers, Beijing investors,

or ascending in warehouse service elevators to vast, pigeon-infested studios,

or developing scent sensitivities in packed auction halls, fanning her nose with a ping-pong paddle, bidding by accident.

Like I say, our girl was busy.

And every day getting a whole lot more dour; her upturned mouth—that iron smile—slowly pulled by gravity towards a flat line; her kinked hair—the canary of her spirit—wilting as though her essential coil was bleeding compression, extension, and torsion.

Activity at the Floss Gallery had pretty much ceased, but that didn't stop people showing up to stare doggedly at the Hours of Operation card posted on the door, complaining to each other how unprofessional it was to list hours that were never kept. Didn't help to call, either. The answering machine's message button blinked day and night, like a beacon to warn low-flying aircraft. The gallery's email inbox reached its limit. Only the Facebook account was active, having become a message board where folks craving connection with the gallery—no matter how remotely—posted images of recent works.

Then came Floss's sudden trip northeast to Montreal, a sojourn announced with a note on the kitchen table (something about helping an Estonian sculptor file for his green card), followed by a whole month of radio silence.

Not a text

not a call

not an email

not a tweet

not a one-winged joual-speaking pigeon with a "hey, how you doin'?" socked to its shin.

Prologue: Part II

Passive-aggressive Budsy on the horn with Floss the night she got back:

"Floss, where the fuck have you been?

I missed you.

Why didn't you call?

I can't wait to see you, put my arms around you.

I missed you so much.

Why didn't you answer my messages?

I was so worried."

Later, we cabbed it to a Midtown rendezvous with Floss in Muldoon's Middlin' Irish Pub, a dank saloon with sizzling neon shamrocks and bolted-down mahogany barstools jammed so tight along the sticky counter that the backrests knocked together when you tried to swivel.

Budsy was ready to rumble. He was wearing the Inquisition's metaphorical red cape. He carried a figurative gym bag stuffed with the carpet of spikes, the garrotte, the branks, and the heretic's fork. He was going to extract some answers.

But savvy Floss straight-armed him immediately, threw him for a loop when she handed each of us a business-class plane ticket and said, "Think Spain. Sunshine. A long bike ride. A reverse pilgrimage."

The effect was like seeing a Rolls-Royce Silver Shadow pull out of a hidden driveway when you've got one eye on a trash compactor making a U-turn and the other on an aggressive cyclist coming up from behind in the inside lane just as a flock of gulls swoops down on a raccoon feasting curbside on a slice of thin-crust pizza. In other words, clever Floss reframed the issue, put more things in play than you could keep a bead on, made it about what she wanted it to be about. Neatly swept under the jute-backed Saxony were all the other questions we'd been burning to ask her. Like where had she been? And what had she done there to make her look so whittled to the quick? And why was she walking like a transformer/Mr. Rodgers, all tentative and stiff?

"A pilgrimage. To Spain."

"That's right. Two weeks. All expenses paid by MiCS."

"What?"

Davy, a small Irishman from County Wexford (so he announced), dressed as a lumberjack and wearing a John Deere baseball cap, butted into our conversation. He was 110 percent certain he had worked with Budsy on a reno (he pronounced it "rinno") up in Yonkers. "Only you weren't called Budsy then."

Belligerent, he insisted on knowing what kind of a name Budsy was, and declaimed to the whole bar that whatever kind of a name it was, it was no kind of name for an Irishman.

"Go away."

"I'm going to," he said. But first he had to tell us how much money he had made and how he was going down to the Dominican Republic to buy a golf course and retire.

"Why are we going to Spain? What for?" I asked.

"Well, John, dear. . ."

"They make tractors," said Wexford. "And I don't work for them. I worked in construction. I told you that. Carpenters Union, Local 608."

"Fuck off."

"We're going to Spain, John, because Floss needs a break," said Floss.

"Another queer bloody name, Floss," said Wexford wheat.

"Ah, give over," said Budsy.

"And what's a reverse pilgrimage?" I asked.

"It's a pilgrimage where you start at the end and you work your way back to the beginning."

"But why would we do that?"

"I once did Lough Derg," said Wexford, removing his John Deere cap and wiping the sweaty strings of his comb-over across the top of his skull. "All night walking in circles saying the rosary in my bare feet with only strong black tea to keep me going. I did Croagh Patrick as well. Later on."

"It would give all of us a change of scene," Floss continued. "Time to figure things out. Budsy, it will give you a chance to unwind, get your head in gear before the big show, which has been rescheduled. We now have a date. Finally. And get this. It's no longer going to be in Chelsea. It's not going to be in London either. It is going to be in Dublin, of all places. Isn't that amazing? You'll be back in the old country. It will be so exciting for you. In MiCS new mansion. The most expensive house in all of Ireland."

"Can I come to Spain with you?" said the Wexford man.

At which point the barman leaned across the counter and told him he was cut off and if he didn't go home he was going to be barred for good.

Prologue: Part III

British Airways from Newark to Dublin, a four-hour stopover in the Irish capital, and then off to Spain.

We so fancy. Enough leg room in business class for Michael Jordan wearing leg braces. Champagne and orange juice in real glass flutes as soon as we sat down. Unlimited refills if we wanted. Only Budsy took that seriously. With a purse of her shimmery lips, the red-hot redhead flight attendant flagged him as a potential problem when he ordered a fourth.

There were five dinner choices. My steak frites arrived on real china, willow pattern, stamped *Wedgewood, by Royal Appointment*. There was serious cutlery as well—heavy stainless steel, sharp where it should be sharp, balanced real nice in the hand.

After the meal, get this, the attendant brought each of us a leatherette case that, among other things, included a light-occluding eye-mask. A black-out bib. Shit, I was Top Cat, reclining in my swank pad. The illusion of class lasted until I attempted to return the mini-valise to the flight attendant before getting off the plane. Yeah. You can take the brother from the ghetto...

In Dublin Airport, Budsy wolfed two fried breakfasts—a tradition, he said—sunny-side-up eggs, tomatoes, sausages, bacon strips shaped like half a flattened pair of aviator shades, the pink lenses pooled with grease, and, to cap it off, some binary racist shit, white pudding and black pudding, all washed down with stainless-steel pots of Barry's tea.

Afterwards, claiming trapped wind, he paced around Terminal 2 like Ted Hughes's jaguar, like Rilke's panther, like Beyoncé behind the defibrillator pad of her pubic bone. Only those who didn't know him would have thought him happy to be back in the country of his birth.

"Every time I come home," he said, "I feel like I'm going against my own grain. Not once but twice: once on arrival and again on departure."

Whatever.

First World problems, like a jam-packed Ryan Air flight to Santiago de Compostela.

Prologue: Part IV

The Spanish cabbie turned out to be Portuguese. He went by the name of Ronaldo. "Like the footballer, yes." He was well-dressed and carefully-groomed, a precise man. He pointed out that we were going about the pilgrimage the wrong way. He said pilgrims usually started off in Saint-Jean-Pied-de-Port in France and ended in Santiago de Compostela. Therefore, he should drive in reverse from the airport into the city.

"Sure thing," Floss said. "Knock yourself out. As long as the meter runs in reverse, too, and you end up paying *us* when we get to the hotel."

We were all a bit cranky from the overnight flight. Dehydrated, tired, and so worried about everything and nothing—this whole idea was stupid, the bastard offspring of drunk thinking. There was so much that could go wrong: how were we going to deal with the language? Would we ever make it home again? Would we get diarrhea?

Three 60-inch flat-screen TV boxes were waiting for us at hotel reception. Our bikes.

The concierge—a greasy dude with one blue eye—gave us the phone number for the person who delivered them and who would custom-assemble them for us. "You call. You call," he said, handing Floss a card, at which she scowled. Like that was going to happen.

Five minutes later, a young Galician in a Clash t-shirt, baseball hat, and denim pencil skirt arrived in the lobby. She spoke with a lisp and only to Floss.

Arrival

Inside Santiago de Compostela Cathedral (Botafumeiro)

You gotta love the language of cathedrals. The botafumeiro (Gali-cian for censer, not to be confused with "fuhgeddaboudit," Brook-lyn for censor) was big as a garbage can. It looked like a silver samovar, or a giant pepper shaker. It hung from the cathedral raf-ters. A host of middle-aged altar boys set it in motion by yanking on a rope. In no time at all, this smoking bomb whipped across the chancel and transept in an arc that must have been two hun-dred degrees. It swung so high it almost hit the ceiling. It threw off heat and filled the vaulted room with saintly smoke.

While the men pulled, an organist played. While the men pulled and the organ played, a nun sang, off-key.

My pew-mate, an ex-priest (Father Cronkite), said the ritual of the botafumeiro went back to medieval times. Pilgrims arriv-ing in Santiago smelled bad—no Speed-Stick back then. Nor were hostels equipped with multi-speed shower nozzles. There were no clean bed sheets. There were no sheets at all—there was straw. And it wasn't clean. As a result, pilgrims arrived rank and fly-bitten from the road, some of them sick. Church incense masked the funk, the unholy trinity of pit rot, crotch fumes, halitosis.

I kept flinching as that thurible (what ex-Father C called it) flew back and forth above us. I felt it gust. Man, it was travelling—a wrecking ball. It was Louis Farrakhan. I kept thinking it was going to go into a speed wobble and sling across the altar, taking out the bishop. Lift him high and splat him like a bluebottle, adding another layer of stain to the stained glass.

"I kept imagining it was filled with hash," Floss said.

"Me, too," said Budsy.

Could be they were on to something. Could be it was toasting a pound of Moroccan blonde. And maybe it was just the swinging motion that made me feel dizzy, sent a landslide of crystals down my inner ear. Dark angels whispered—was this mass hypnosis?

I left my pew, stepped out into the narthex, where an old woman in black paced in prayer, repeatedly kissing the feet of the crucifix she held before her. Eleven times she puckered and pecked smackingly while I recovered under the Portico of Glory, admiring the carving of St. James on the central mullion, the saints and evangelists pogo-ing on jambs above piers and pilasters, the ox and the lion and a host of other figures ranged across the tympanum—the scene so crowded that I started to feel claustrophobic and had to step outside for some air and low-key aerobics.

I jogged across the courtyard, flailing my arms, working my head from side to side. I made a yawn mouth until my mandibles clicked reset. Adrian! I raised my brows until, with a crunch, my skull lifted off my spine before settling back into bobble position. My vertigo drained away.

By then I was far enough back that I could take in the whole Romanesque-Baroque disaster of the Cathedral of Santiago de Compostela's façade and towers.

It looked like pictures of the Khmer temple of Angkor Wat.

Outside Santiago de Compostela Cathedral

In shorts, sunhats, and shades, with their clamshells and walking sticks, the pilgrims arrived at the cathedral.

Like sea creatures suddenly pulled up on land; most of them didn't seem to know what to do now that they'd reached the end. It was understandable. Who knows how long the Camino had been a spiritual beacon in their lives? How it helped them cope with dirty jobs, comatose marriages, toxic children, sudden death, leaking faith, disease, or any of the other thousand humiliations and degradations that attach by sucker mouth to siphon the soul dry in the course of lifetimes that are increasingly too long.

All the more tragic then, when completion turned out to be a deficit.

More grim faces than happy ones. On the whole, a lot of disappointed brothers wandering the courtyard. Some had ants in their pants. Mexican jumping beans in their cotton socks. St. Vitus breakdancers, they couldn't stop moving and flexing. Others were downright angry. One group, led by a box-jawed priest, came hoisting a ten-foot cross with a life-sized fiberglass Jesus they'd carried all the way from Pamplona. The priest looked like he'd been expecting banners and flags, crowds lining the streets waving olive branches, a posse of cardinals applauding, he looked like he'd been expecting the Pope to present him with some Vatican medal of honour.

He took his disappointment out on the poor people selling souvenirs, those offering to buy back walking sticks and sea shells.

Jesus in the temple.

Shit. I thought that priest was going to whip out an Uzi from under his robe and spray the whole place. He was in a Scarface fucking rage. *Come and meet my little frien'.*

"I guess after such a long walk, the endpoint is anticlimactic." Floss said.

We were sitting outside a café just off the main courtyard, drinking milky coffee, taking it all in. I was eating an almond croissant every bit as stale as the ones I used to serve from Baby Bilbao back home.

"Like the last day of summer camp," said Budsy, looking up from his guide book.

"How's it like summer camp?"

Budsy was ramped up, fully caffeinated. "The way I see it, these pilgrims have been together all day every day for weeks. In the same bunkhouses at night. They've just shared the highs and lows of an eight hundred kilometre walk. They've all pursued a common goal in an unfamiliar place. They've had the chance to find themselves and to present their findings to the world. Think of the Camino as a sandbox. A chance to leave old habits behind. Maybe it worked. Maybe for the duration of the walk, it all came together sweetly. They made new friends, they had some great experiences, et cetera. . . Now all of a sudden they are in Santiago, the terminal point of the pilgrimage. They got that final stamp on their pilgrim passports. Some are happy. Some are not happy. Some get drunk. But really, they are jonesing. Even the happy ones. Something is missing. It's not until they board the bus to go home that it hits them. Maybe all that newfound intimacy? That openness? Maybe it wasn't as authentic as they thought it was. The complications of the life left behind begin to reassert themselves; the old patterns to overwhelm more recent resolutions. One thought leads to another: a sneaking suspicion that none of it was really real. Logic overwhelms faith. If they can't even get on board the bus with their resurrected souls intact, what hope do they have of keeping it all alive back in the real world. Y'know?"

"They had summer camp over in Ireland?" Floss said.

"I didn't say that. I'm drawing from my knowledge of Hollywood films."

"Too bleak, Budsy," Floss said. "Take that English woman on the steps. The one who was crying. I asked her what was the matter and she hugged me. I mean she really hugged me. She told me the last month changed her life. She was no longer the same person. She said she loved herself for the first time in her life. She said it all came from a sense that she was not doing the Camino for herself. Her pilgrimage became hers only when she understood why she was doing it. She said she walked with the dead and for the dead. Every day she walked through her pain and was sustained by the thought of all those who could not make the journey, who had died or who were too sick to attempt it. "I did it for them," she said. "It wasn't about me. And in the process I became a different person from the one who began the journey."

"People always say that," said Budsy.

"Say what?"

"People who want to change themselves always say 'I am not the same person now as I was back then.' But what they're actually doing is remembering how they *felt* back then. Not how they presented themselves. When you remember the past, you remember how you really were—not how you were pretending to be at the time. The same principle applies in the here and now, but it's reversed. "Changed people" present themselves as being changed but they don't tell you how they're really feeling inside. They mightn't be feeling half as changed as they say they are. It's all *fake it 'til you make it*. Believing in the vision does not make it true."

"You're a cynic."

"Maybe, but I'm not alone."

"You pointing the finger?"

"I am, but not at you."

"Who then?"

"That little bollocks in the Compostela office. Remember? All those eager-beaver pilgrims queued up to get their completion certificate. And him treating them like they were getting tickets to a movie. I mean most of them had just walked right across Spain."

"Now that you bring it up, Budsy," I said, "Why did you want us to get pilgrim passports? It's not like you're a believer."

"I thought I might be able to use mine for artistic purposes. Part of a collage, maybe. Or, if I manage to get all the stamps, I can sell the passport on eBay. There's bound to be some mutt out there who's trying to get back into the good graces of his Catholic wife: 'Look, honey, I did penance. I walked a thousand miles for you. Busted my balls.'"

First Day

The Apostle John on the First Day

I was all up for the medieval. I was down for some Iberian vibes. I was all for going on the road, getting back in touch with my nomadic side. I was down with that beat. Not even the rain could dampen my spirit.

And it rained real hard our first day in Spain. I mean it pelted all through the hills—we were nowhere near the plain. Stucco on puddles. A fuzz of moisture on the road's potholed asphalt. Drizzle-mist ascended into the atmosphere when the downpour let up, which it did intermittently, like it was tired of carrying its own load.

"It's only vertical rain," said Budsy. "In Ireland the rain comes at you sideways to the perpendicular all day every day for eleven of the twelve months of the year."

To prove his manliness, he left his waterproof poncho packed away in the bottom of his knapsack, betting the shower would soon stop. He bet on the hot Spanish sun drying it before it fell all the way down. Budsy liked to phrase things in a way that blew past the stupid listener and made the intelligent groan.

Next Stop: Los Lobos

"Next stop, Los Lobos," Budsy roared, powering alongside us. He meant O Laboreiro, which was about the halfway point for that day, and where we had agreed to rendezvous if separated. He flew past, his back tire arcing a fine spray, grit and mud skunking his orange overalls from butt to shoulder blades.

If the weather was a spur to him, it was a downer for me. Water had already penetrated my Gore-Tex. My clothes were beginning to sponge. The wedge-shaped saddle was starting to chafe. My spirit was the tiniest Bic flame trying to brown the edges of my increasingly waterlogged will (evidence of which can found in my road journal). To make matters worse, my metaphors were becoming intolerable.

"O Laboreiro!" I shouted at him.

Just as he was about to pull ahead, Floss, standing in her stir-rups, decided to play Gandalf to his Balrog, swerving out in front of him. You shall not pass! She wanted to tease, not bait him. But the pit bulls of his temperament lunged, reared up on their haunches, their big jaw muscles bulging.

There was friction between him and Floss. It was hard to miss. A little bit of grit had intruded between their gliding parts. And it had been there for some time.

I would go as far as to say—hell, let me just say it straight: the grit blew in thirteen months earlier, the night MiCS made his appearance in DUMBO. It was rooted in the weight of expecta-tion the big man dumped on us. Expectation that went mostly unmet.

The Chelsea show he promised Budsy had not materialized, though space was booked and marketing begun. Budsy, who—at least in theory—was working hard on his secret installation, could at least point to the MiCS website if cornered by some competitive double-A (Asshole Artist) at a party. "It's coming, dude. You don't have to take my word for it. Check online."

Yeah, there was friction between them alright. And travelling together didn't help. The change in scene was finding fault lines, and these surfacing obstacles were steering Budsy and Floss to a field of dreams sewn with landmines.

Budsy was nervous about being in Spain. And Floss wasn't in

the mood to coddle him. As far as she was concerned, Budsy was being a big pussy.

"Follow the yellow arrows;" she called out to him, "they mark the trail."

The Reverse Pilgrimage

Not that it was a hard path to follow with the constant stream of pilgrims coming at us. Who'd have counted on so many in October? But there they were in ones and twos. With their walking sticks and clamshells. With their rain gear. With their shorts and sensible shoes. All different but all the same. Their sartorial choices spread the news. Some were in big priest-led groups and wore matching bandanas—reds and blues were the most common, though one group wore faded yellow with brown polka dots, like the skins of overripe bananas. Most of them looked mighty happy with themselves, like they just won at bingo. Some sang hymns in the kind of high, warbly voices you hear in white churches the world over. Some wore windbreakers with crucifix logos. Many were Spaniards or southern Europeans. A few were limping along, looking broken inside from the long walk. I expected to see more of the limping types after what I'd seen the day before at the Santiago cathedral. More than a few of them hailed me, wanted to stop and talk. Others glared resentfully at us as we rode in the opposite direction. Like we should move over and give them the road. Like they didn't dig the reverse-pilgrimage idea, didn't relish the contradiction.

Floss on the First Day

Floss sold the trip to Budsy by appealing to the basal node of his brain, the bit that Venn diagrams with the top of his spine, the ancient trough where thinking takes a spa day to brine in the body's salts. She told him time in the Spanish sticks would give him time to work out the details of his big show for MiCS. Not that he thought there was anything to work out, or that he needed the time to do it. Motherfucker rambled through life thinking all he had to do was imagine shit to make it happen. All he needed, he said, was a week to prep the site; easy access to a purveyor of wild game (Floss: What kind of game?); a light show (Floss: LED or lasers?); a dozen deep freezes (Floss: Would fridges do? Would ice suffice in a pinch?); and a couple good carpenters (Floss: Do they really have to be union?)

Floss knew the list would expand like impetigo the closer to the date we got. She knew Budsy would panic, wobble, crash, revive, and be in need of support. She'd be there with caffeine, Xanax, and alcohol. She'd work the phones. Bring it on.

Possible Root Cause

Floss knew better than anyone that you could never believe what Budsy-man said when he was gearing up for a show. It wasn't that he lied. Not exactly. He just didn't know. Diplomat Floss would say he lacked self-awareness. When Budsy's pain was gone? There'd never been any pain. When he was happy? He'd *always* been happy. Budsy was a child whose inner child still wore—his word—a nappy. Budsy's one of those helpless, charming types that women just pick up after.

Floss blamed his mother. Yeah, I know, the mother is always to blame. But in his case? Totally true. You only had to look in his eyes when he talked about his saintly dead mammy, run over by a tractor outside the town of Ballinasloe just months before Budsy puddle-jumped to New York at the tender age of twenty.

According to Budsy, his ma waited on him hand and foot. Dinner was always on the table when he came in. His shirts were always ironed—hell, she even ironed his jeans. As far as his mama was concerned, he was perfect. She never criticized the little princeling. She *doted*—his word—on Budsy so much he reached the point where he started to expect everyone else to do the same. He acted like his presence was spotlit and whatever he did should get a round of applause.

Weird thing was? He hated being on the stage. Budsy was happiest behind the scenes, most comfortable on the page.

What the Apostle J Thought about Reverse Engineering the Pilgrim's Way

I was genuinely jazzed, pumped about going to Spain. I did a little Mr. Bojangles soft-shoe number right in the middle of Muldoon's when Floss floated the idea. High-fived every raised hand. Low-fived a few, too. I grew up with a lot of Latinos on Staten Island. Even had a few words of Spanish.

"*No dejes para mañana lo que puedas hacer hoy.*" (Translation: Don't put off until tomorrow what you can do today). "*No fíes mujer de fraile, ni barajes con alcade*" (Translation: A king's favour is no inheritance)—ya, MiCS, I'm talking about you.

At the same time, I wasn't really buying Floss's whole reverse-pilgrimage story. It left a tang of decoy paint on my tongue; it was subterfuge, a deluge of ideas designed to mask the truth that all was not right in the State of Floss.

This wasn't just LGBTQ, it was KGB, too. The girl had moves. She always had some hidden agenda. Not that I was going to press her about what she was concocting this time. Floss had natural-born leader genes, which meant she needed respect. No problem. If that's what she needed, that's what I'd give her. I never asked her about her private life—she guarded that one like she was the NSA. I let her think I accepted her at face value.

Do you know how rare that is? Especially in the tri-state area? Motherfuckers where I grew up were always up in your grill— mouthy mansplainers and womansplainers, always demanding their rights, wanting to know why: Why you like everything bagels? Why you don't drive? (they look at me like I should be wearing a helmet); and when they run out of whys they go to whats: What's your name anyway? What's a guy like me doing in their neighbourhood? Subtext understood.

Respected, Floss gave the same back. In her eyes—and she was one of the few—I was black, no question about it. So I wasn't going to turn over that apple cart. I wasn't going to ask anybody about whatever troubles she was having with Budsy. Nuh-uh. I wasn't going to complain. I wasn't about to point out that if anyone had suffered from our involvement with MiCS, it was me and me only. I wasn't about to spill about feeling like a fifth wheel.

What Floss and I Had in Common

We both grew up on Staten Island: me around New Dorp, on the strip between Hyland Boulevard and the ocean, and Floss farther down, at Huguenot, right near Richmond Town, where old George Washington rode his piebald pony hard, drumming up support for the Revolution, charming the colonists with his dazzling birchbark smile.

We lived in railway rooms, me and my single-mother mama, Dymphna. My Dominican daddy was long gone. He'd slunk back to Santo Domingo or wherever—Santiago de Los Caballeros, La Romana, Punta Cana—back to some Island shithole—soon after I was born.

I never spoke to anyone about my dad. I didn't talk much about my childhood either, though thinking about it could make me feel lowdown, not depressed exactly, more like melancholy or—what's the word?—*forlorn*, yeah, that's closer. I didn't yelp about my hard-knock life. I also refused the pharmaceutical solutions on offer. I didn't buy into psychology and therapy-quackery—just organized religion by another name.

Floss told me I was stoical. She told me I got that from my Irish mama.

Turns out she was right. The last thing my mama said to me every night before she turned out the light was: "Don't be a whiner, Johnny. Nobody's gonna like you if you whine."

I think about my mama all the time.

Budsy Pulls Ahead on the First Day

"Fuck Spain.
Fuck the rain in Spain.
Fuck the Spanish.
Fuck the idea of coming here and fuck Floss for having the idea.
Fuck her for pretending it was her idea in the first place.
Fuck MiCS whose invisible hand is in all of this.
Fuck John for playing along and fuck me for letting myself half
   believe them.
Fuck my bike and its twenty-six gears.
Fuck the man who invented it.
Fuck the up-and-down road.
Fuck the green hills and the eucalyptus trees.
Fuck Galicia and the incomprehensible Spanish they speak here.
Fuck the Celtic influence, the round stone huts with thatched roofs.
Fuck the first fifty kilometres.
Fuck that bike saddle rubbing my taint. Fuck those who say a
   man doesn't have a taint.
Fuck the red mud and the grit running up my back.
Fuck the pilgrims with their sticks and leisure clothes.

Fuck the plain sticks. Fuck the carved sticks. Fuck the hip-high sticks and fuck the chin-high staffs.

Fuck Gandalf and fuck Moses.

Fuck the scallop shells and fuck the horse that bolted into the sea, nearly drowning its rider.

Fuck Saint James for saving them.

Fuck the stone boat he travelled in.

Fuck no oars and fuck no sail.

Fuck the dumb scallop shells stuck all over the horse when it bolted back out of the ocean.

Fuck the rider for surviving. Fuck him for thinking he was saved.

Fuck the origin of myth.

Fuck the shitty little student in the Compostela office handing out pilgrimage certificates and stamps like they were aspirins; the bored locals for thinking we were pilgrims; the cathedral and that big swinging censer; the sweaty funk; the mania and depression for presenting as spiritual revelation; fuck John for slipping away with that woman and getting laid; Floss for pretending she was into me in that way, then flirting with the bike girl, thinking she could fool me; fuck hormones, laser hair removal and reconstructive surgery; fuck gender-neutral pronouns. Fuck them.

And Fuck Micks.

Especially fuck MiCS.

Fuck the no-show in New York.

Fuck the no-show in London.

Fuck Dublin.

And fuck me if MiCS's Irish mansion doesn't seem perfect for my new installation.

Fuck the most expensive house in all of Ireland.

Fuck its balcony overlooking the expansive foyer.

Fuck MiCS for being right.

Fuck me for being bought.

Fuck me for being disagreeable.

Fuck the first day in Spain and the nine more to come.

Fuck 750 more kilometres.
Fuck being with people.
Fuck everyone."

Lunch in O Laboreiro

Whitewashed walls with black-and-white photographs of immigrants, maybe from the nineteenth century and the last wave of religio-hoofers between the end of the ancient pilgrimage and its revival in the 1970s. Red gingham tablecloths. Ashtrays. Galicia was Europe's smoking section. A wall of foreign currency notes behind the small bar. A picture of Padre Pio. There was also a collection of walking sticks for sale, a pair of snowshoes, and what looked to be a well-stocked first-aid section between the vodka and the potato chips.

The place had the cloying stench of chemical cleaners.

"You are Americans."

"Si," said Budsy.

"You come on a very good day. Today we have two specials. The first it is a white fish stew, which is our specialty. The second it is *pulpo a la gallega*. Fresh today."

"Pulpo," said Budsy, "does that mean mashed?"

"No, señor. Is octopus slices served on pieces of potato. Spicy with paprika. My favourite. Very delicious."

"Mmmh. I'll have the octopus," said Budsy. "And three Heineken."

"I'll have the same," I said, "But not three Heineken."

"Of course. And for the lady?"

"I think I'll just have some bread. And no Heineken for me, hon. Just water."

"Bread and water. The diet of saints," said Budsy.

"Speaking of saints," Floss said, "those people outside were *so* wanting to talk. They called me over as soon as I pulled into the square. This German woman—"

"I know what you mean," said Budsy. "Every second person who passed me going the opposite way this morning wanted to stop and chat. Asked where I was from. Told me where they were coming from, how long they'd been on the road, et cetera. Even worse—they wanted to tell me *why* they were on the road. Most of them had about as much English as I have Spanish. It was comical at times. All of them were in some sort of a crisis. A lad from Portsmouth whose girlfriend just dumped him. A woman from Switzerland making the pilgrimage because her sick parents asked her to do it for them. They asked her 'to take ze hike.'"

"The only people I spoke to," I said, "were two sisters from Australia. One of them was squatting behind a bush and her friend was on lookout. They were power-walking from León to Santiago. Said they wanted a vacation with no beaches and no hangovers. Of course they also asked me why I was making the pilgrimage and why I was going the wrong way."

"What did you say?"

"Said I hadn't figured that out yet."

"I just told people I wanted to lose weight," said Budsy.

"The Germans outside," Floss continued, "the little plump lady with the pink windbreaker said she left her house in Berlin three months ago and walked all the way here. Can you imagine? She walked all across Germany, through France, and then right across Spain.

She said she just turned fifty and felt like emptiness was her birthday present.

A big box of nothing.

She didn't know why, exactly. Said she hadn't lost anyone. There'd been no major changes in her life. But she couldn't shake the feeling. She decided to take the pilgrimage after she saw a documentary about it.

She just had a hunch that walking would make things clearer somehow."

Second Day

The Apostle John on the Second Day

Goddamn my muscles! Vastus-Vastus-Vastus-Rectus! My quad-riceps were the strings on Sid Vicious's bass when I stretched my legs that second day. My whole body had an erection. The S&M burn as I pushed up the hill, turning the pedals that turned the chain that turned the wheel, layer upon layer of resistance, the globe spinning underneath in the opposite direction.

The only way out was through. But real slow.

Goddamn the ripped muscle trying to heal! The frayed meat fabric trying to knit. Stitch in my side. Tugging sensation in the back of my neck. Stomach so queasy, I felt like puking.

I was thinking about the grey-haired woman I'd walked back to her hotel. Near-Birmingham-Angie. NBA from Alabama. How could I forgive her racism? I could not. But I could get onside with her efforts to set things right. Tell her she was on a long, hard road. Keep at it, keep your goal in sight. That's what I'd said back in the tavern—well, intimated more than said—and told her she'd eventually get to see the mountain.

She took my hand and invited me back to her room. Said she wanted to share her body with me. To meet Jesus in that way. Hey, who am I to question the workings of the Holy Spirit?

Biceps Femoris-Semimembranosus-Senitendinosus! The extinct dinosaurs of my hamstrings restrung as I cycled the first half mile out of Sarria, all of it up a steep hill.

Thoughts of Angie with me.

Scent of Angie on me.

Who knew an older body could be that exciting?

Not as fleshy, true.

More sinew.

Closer to the bone.

Toned and tanned after her pilgrimage.

Such a luxurious mitt of hair.

Down there.

No vertical Mohawk, edged in goosepimpled rough.

She shook. She trembled. Told me the pilgrimage had been an awakening on many levels. For the first time in her life, she said, she felt truly sexual. Told me she had three different lovers between the Pyrenees and Santiago de Compostela. I asked her if that hurt but she didn't get the joke. Said she was going to meet up with the second guy back in the States. Before that, there'd only ever been her ex-husband, a real brute. And now there was me. So beautiful your skin, your smell, your hair, she kept saying.

I'd been there before. The whole black-on-white thing. Her first time with a brother. No Spanish fly like taboo. But this time was different. She just came and came. Cried and came. Came again. Cried some more. Like she was in the middle of some kind of breakdown or breakthrough.

The crucifix around her neck tapped against her breastbone: 35 rpm by my count. It was like I wasn't there. She threw her head back, stared heavenward. I was a bucking bronco bringing her to the Lord.

Gastrocnemius-Soleus-Plantaris! How my calf muscles hardened as I approached the summit of the hill. Yoyo Ma bowing hard on my Achilles tendon. Resonance.

Alabama Angie, the hard-bodied fifty-year-old racist. In one night, she had expanded, if not redrawn, the map of my desire.

Gluteus maximus-obliques-serratus! The pleasure in that pain.

I was over the hill and there was so much to look forward to.

There was Floss ahead of me, just about visible through curtains of rain.

The Apostle John Scores

It's complicated. The point of my story is this: on my way back from Angie's hotel, I spotted our bike girl—the babe in the Clash t-shirt—the señorita who flirted with Floss. She was smoking a doob with some friends. So I stopped and asked if they had any to sell. Purchased a thumbnail-size piece of red hash for way too much cash. Helena—that was her name—told me this was good stuff: "goood for moocèll pain."

Floss on the Second Day: Deep Muscle Memory

Floss drank in the looks of the Spanish men as she rode out of Santiago de Compostela that second morning. So many gorgeous men with such adoring eyes. So full of lust and sin. And it wasn't only the locals who ogled her, looked at her as if she were bull's meat tenderized by adrenaline. More than a few holy pilgrims bingo-dabbed their souls with pitch by making a one-eighty to take in that splendid rear view: Floss's butt all teed up on a tiny saddle.

Who better than Floss to know what men were like? She could turn at the exact right moment to catch an ogle. She had a woman-plus sense about eyeballing. How couldn't she? She felt the moth-weight of every male gaze as it landed on her. She was rarely blindsided.

Her spandex bike suit clung—its design a bizarre palette of thick trowel smears: reds, blues, purples, and yellows. Made her body look flayed, like a textbook diagram of human musculature. But it showed off everything the way Floss wanted it to be shown. Streetwise Missy was all coy and flirtatious. Unbelievable. I kept catching her posing as if there were telephoto lenses pointing at her from all points of the compass. Voguing. Classic airhead exhibitionist stuff. But sweet, too, in its own way. She was dazzled by her own reflection. She'd fallen in love.

Maybe.

She was thinking with her little head.

Probably.

Floss on the Second Day: Memory 1

By hour four on the road, back muscles corseting from the strain of the steady uphill, Floss had been gaffed back into the flux of distant times: fishing with her dad on the Jersey shore. It was what her father did to unwind from his job in insurance.

He wore khaki shorts and shirt, zip-up vest with net pockets. He even had one of those flowerpot hats with the floppy brim, lures stuck all over it. Aviator shades and a plastic-filtered cigar rounded out the ensemble. Total nerd—you knew at a glance. Even at eight years old, Floss found her father's outfits hilarious.

And she did *not* like baiting a fish hook—earthworms and bacon strung like Fourth of July bunting on triple barbs—worm texture like chin bristle. Get a grip, she told herself, pushing against the feeling that this cruel act was somehow damaging something inside her. She did it anyway. She wanted to please her daddy.

Her father pretended to be tough, but he didn't like baiting hooks either. "Fuck," he shouted out, when an enormous purple-headed nightcrawler wrapped around his wrist. Afterwards, he apologized to her for the bad language.

Floss complained, too, about the revolting raw chicken they used to bait crab pots. Pimply white skin flapping from the bone; the shiny, plastic-looking purple flesh underneath. She made as if to barf in a display of exaggerated disgust.

And she cried on the day she saw a seagull dive and gobble up a spinner—the bird torn from the sky by some jerk who thought its distress was hysterical, who kept letting it go so he could reel it back in.

Floss on the Second Day: Memory 2

When she was thirteen, Floss developed a serious crush on a jock, Pat O'Sullivan, a leggy, broad-shouldered eighth-grader with blow-dried, flipped-back hair parted in the middle, like Scott Baio. His mother was from Yonkers. His father was from Idaho.

Floss was still in seventh grade, the precinct of acne, shadow moustaches, blushes, bullies, masturbation, and eating disorders. Pat was that critical step ahead, just entering the precinct of the cool, the beginnings of know-how and the insane confidence to execute it. Plus he was a football player (a receiver) and pole vaulter on the track and field team.

To impress Pat, middle-school Floss made the volleyball squad. She played for his attention—not that he ever came to the games. He probably never even knew her name. He was too busy humping space invaders down at the arcade, or getting handjobs from Sheila Darjeeling under the bleachers on the south side of the lacrosse field.

Lying in her bedroom at night, Floss pictured him in the locker room, a white towel around his waist; the same locker room where Floss dressed and undressed like a girl, under a bath towel her mother had converted into a poncho by cutting a neck-hole in the centre.

Before falling asleep, Floss prayed to the god she didn't believe in that Pat would show up just once to watch her play.

He didn't.

She won a trophy for him. She brought it home. Her dad was so happy, he got drunk and offered her a beer. They placed the trophy on the mantle. Her already happy mom was even happier. She jogged in place and clapped her hands like a toddler. She brought out Floss's golden Terminator 2 figure whenever anybody came over.

Coincidentally or not, Floss figured out—around the same time she knew for sure that Pat O'Sullivan had never been and never would be interested in her—that she never had, and never would, want him the way a boy wants another boy. She pictured herself as Olivia Newton-John in *Grease*, the debutante version, not the leatherette vixen.

Floss on the Second Day: Memory 3

Big shout-out to the Huguenot branch of the New York Public Library.

Huguenot: out-of-the-way hamlet where sleepy snakes wound out of the grass onto the sidewalk, where unsupervised gangs of kids flicked them high in the air with sticks.

Huguenot: two-street village with one pizza place that served a dynamite thin slice, cheese with sprinkled chili flakes—big Dino behind the counter—where they went after school for events or to celebrate the start of summer holidays.

Huguenot: where there were no bars. Instead, there was a single fine-dining restaurant where they went on special occasions, like Floss's birthday.

Huguenot: where it was great to be a kid because the inhabitants were either Italian or Irish. Two halves of the same brass-mouthed population that said children should be seen and not heard, but didn't believe it, not for a New York minute. These were refugees from the tenements of Brooklyn and downtown Manhattan. For them, this place, just across the bridge (the Guinea gangplank) was something close to a countryside heaven.

Huguenot: where, best of all, there was the branch library just one block from Floss's house—clearly the work of some ambitious councillor who'd since moved on to bigger and better things.

Floss always waxed poetic—she almost sang—when she talked about the Huguenot library. If you knew her, you would know how outside her comfort zone poetry lived. "The place was a rope ladder that fell from the clouds and landed at my feet."

To this day, Floss donates to the NYPL. If her contributions have kept up with her earnings, it's safe to say she may one day have a branch or a collection named after her.

She still flaps on about walking up the concrete ramp to the front door. For Floss, this wasn't just a one-room library with two computers, a photocopier, and books on shelves (most of them bestsellers)—this was a portal to a whole other world.

"Kudos to whoever ordered *Mom, I Need to Be a Girl,*" she said.

She still talks about Diane, the world's greatest librarian, who brought in books for her from branches all over the city—from Baychester to Tottenville. "Diane was a doll. A living doll," Floss says, "and she had the best nails."

Floss on the Second Day: Memory 4

Her first counsellor, X, had wet brown eyes. Their expression reminded Floss of a donkey that had spent its whole life in one field and from the burden of its isolation and confinement had developed sensitivity for the private struggles of every other living thing. This donkey wore grey flannel suits and black polo necks. It had a firm handshake.

They confirmed Floss was not a freak. "You must never think of yourself that way," they said. "To think of yourself in that way is a..." Floss could tell they wanted to use the word *sin*, but couldn't quit dig it out of the lead-lined box where that word got stashed on the first day of graduate school. The counsellor laid out some options. "For treatment?" moms asked her after that day's session. "For treatment?" she asked again when Floss didn't answer.

X put Floss in touch with the Mazzoni Center in Philadelphia. Why Philly? To this day, Floss doesn't know. Maybe it was the only clinic in their Rolodex. It wasn't until Floss made her escape to the city that she realized there were better services much closer to home.

Floss on the Second Day: Memory 5

Grandma Lopez laid out in a casket in a funeral home near Hazlet, a strip-mall hamlet near Exit 17 in New Jersey. Grandma with her rosary beads wrapped around her bony hands, purple veins and capillaries visible through her skin. All her impishness mysteriously vanished.

Floss was real upset because she loved her grandma and because in death the funeral home had dressed her in her granniest outfit (beige cardigan over a pink floral dress) and not in the chartreuse Chanel suit she treasured above all else and wore at every special event for as long as Floss could remember. The family photo albums will corroborate.

Then, surprise of surprises, next day there was a phone call from her grandma's lawyer, a Mister Rivera from the Bronx. This nice man told her that he had known her grandmother for over forty years; he said they used to jitterbug together at the Savoy. *That* Floss could believe. He then told her about a second secret will in which she left Floss an amazing sum of money.

Her parents never knew how much.

A week later, Floss is gone, towing two gym bags. First to the YWCA ("Do you have a vacancy for a back scrubber?"—she was so excited), and then—through sheer luck—she found her rent-controlled place at 23rd and 9th.

Floss on the Second Day: Memory 6

Floss spent her first years in New York working as a home-care provider. She now looks back on that job and that whole period as an expression of her uncertain mental condition. She just wanted to do good. She wanted to make recompense. She wanted to hide. She was as pious as a Catholic girl on the threshold of adolescence.

Floss's employer was an Upper East Side grande dame, one Mrs. Pearl Goldberg. Sixteenth floor with a view of the Park, the apartment swank, but rundown, way below shabby chic. There was filth. Crud on the baseboards, hairballs big as subway rats. But with blinds permanently drawn and low-watt bulbs on dim, the decay was kept under wraps.

Floss was one of three home-care workers who came every day, each one working an eight-hour shift. Caregivers, care-workers, home care, personal assistants—the label depended on the agency. The whole thing was a scam. Most of them cared only about cleaning out the old lady's fridge and stealing her Percocet. They kept her sedated. They turned her over, changed her diapers, or brought her a bedpan when she needed to do number two.

Three years Floss looked after the old lady, mostly taking the night shift. Visitors were few. Mrs. G's hairdresser, Carmine, came on the first Tuesday of every month to tint her fiery mane an even more incendiary shade of red. He came late, only after the salon had closed. He made her laugh. He told her she was beautiful. She told him he was full of shit. He told her she needed to get laid. She made as if to throw back the covers. It was their trusted vaudeville routine.

Mrs. Goldberg's son, Barry, a lawyer, visited on Fridays to bring groceries and trays of Lego-coloured prescription pills. The medication kept her alive. Or half alive. It was an existence.

Barry, in Floss's words, was a total shit-heel. He told Floss right off that he thought there was something not quite right about her. He told her he was keeping an eye on her, a real close eye. Six weeks later, he was asking her out. He was bringing flowers and boxes of chocolates for Floss when he carried in the food and pills for his mother.

"No mother deserves such a son," Floss said. "No one should end up living alone in an apartment with the drapes permanently drawn."

Floss couldn't say what kept the old lady going. Memories, maybe.

When lucid, Pearl Goldberg told Floss the same stories over and over. She talked about Frank and Ava, Ava and Frank. The jazz clubs around Midtown after the war.

And her honeymoon up in the Canadian Rockies in a big hotel with a green lake and bears wandering all around.

Floss on the Second Day: Memory 7

Pearl Goldberg's dead husband, Schlomo, liked to wheel and deal in art. "I had no time for it," Mrs. G told Floss. "Music was *my* thing. I was crazy for jazz, for the great singers—Ella, Blossom, Sarah, Dinah, Nina, and my favourite, Billie. Oh that marvellous Billie! I saw them all, too many times to count. They had such hard lives. It wasn't fair. There is no fairness in this world."

Thanks to Schlomo's proclivities, the bedroom library had floor-to-ceiling shelves stacked with art books, auction catalogues, history books, and artist biographies. Floss really got into it. Up in that apartment overlooking the park, she learned everything there was to know about modern art. There were even business files—three large cabinets—in an alcove off the bathroom, folders of appraisal reports, invoices, receipts. But none of the paintings listed among Mr. Goldberg's many acquisitions were in the apartment. Floss checked the storage room, under the beds, and in the closets. She double-checked the paper trail, but still couldn't solve the puzzle. Finally, she asked Mrs. G. about it. The old lady didn't answer, though she appeared to be giving the question a great deal of thought. Floss could see the algorithms running behind Mrs. Goldberg's introspective gaze and suspected what the old woman knew but wasn't saying—Barry had taken the paintings as an appetizer, an early taste of his inheritance.

During those long nights with Mrs. Goldberg, Floss approached her reading as if she were learning a trade. She decided to make art appreciation a part of her new identity. It wasn't just a rational

decision, mechanically executed—she loved it, too. Studying art
was never a chore. She had a natural feel for it. She knew when
critics were right and when they were wrong. In a way, it all came
easy to her. That's because Floss already possessed what could *not*
be learned. She had taste. It was already inside her, just waiting for
the right materials to bring it to the surface. She accepted this gift
as one of her life's few consolations.

Floss on the Second Day: Memory 8

Bleary-eyed at dawn, pulling open the heavy drapes in the dining room to watch the sun come up over Central Park. Watching
the vampires and ghouls leave the cover of darkness for the toxic
light of day. The bulldoggers and their chapstick companions;
yard boys servicing the wrinkle room; girl scouts and Grimm's
fairies, all bagged from a night of rumpy-rumpy and bumper-
to-bumper. Not that she was like them. She didn't feel the need
to hide.

And not that she was judging them.

She should be such a hypocrite.

Floss on the Second Day: Memory 9

Night shift over but not ready for sleep, she'd hit the department
stores and boutiques early in the morning, just as they were opening up, and head straight for the cosmetics counter.

It was all poetry to Floss.

Flip-top moons of shepherd's warning and shepherd's delight
blush displayed on the counter, or stacked underneath like doll's
house plates and saucers.

Shimmering moth-wing foundation.

Anthracite eyeliner.

Petri dishes filled with white beach sand and Sahara-yellow sand.

As she dabbled into the magic potions, Floss tried not to think of civet cats in cages, cherry-eyed bunnies with their little white heads protruding from mini iron-maidens.

Cosmetics-counter etiquette was meted out with a civility rarely found anywhere else in the city—shop assistants who suspected Floss wasn't a woman said nothing. They were only too glad to help. "You're not from around here," they'd say (while handing her a makeup sponge), as a way of starting up a conversation with this stranger who had just jabbed her finger into a rectangle of green eyeshadow.

She worshipped these geishas in labcoats for whom beauty was a science. Their regimens and rituals filled in so many missing pieces—they embodied a real-life version of the Barbie world she'd longed for as a child.

They watched her hover at the fragrance counter, studied her as she inhaled those airy precisions, the aura and balm of bouquet, pheromone incense, the redolent essence of scent like a bon mot on the tip of the tongue, high notes of lemon and lime, of reviving strawberry, with base notes of mold, mildew, and rot.

The acrid, sweet, fetid, crisp, dirty femininity of it all. The fishy florals, the moist loams, the stink of skunk.

Here was the truth. Right under her nose: femininity was all bricks and mortar.

Floss Rants

"Those freakin' Spaniards! What's their problem? There must have been fifty of us in that dorm and they had to close all the windows? Even the shutters? The air was thick. The air was like rancid butter. I could taste what they had for supper. Disgusting.

And the snoring. And then the banging around when they got up this morning. I swear some of them got up at four o'clock. Jesus, when I think of the pious talk around the supper table last night. They can all just eat me. God, it's so bizarre when people who haven't smiled for years suddenly start smiling. You didn't notice? They looked like their faces had cracked open. They looked like fuckin' *Muppets*."

What Budsy Would Never Say about Floss

Emotionally, Floss was a lot like a guy.
　　Her finer feelings tended to get warped into anger.
　　Rage was her steel, to which her finer feelings alloyed,
　　like carbon, manganese, nickel, chromium,
　　　　molybdenum, vanadium, silicon, and boron.
　　Not that some women can't be like that,
　　but it's usually a man thing, moron.

How Budsy and I Met Floss

Muldoon's the night of the Hirst show. The place was packed with every kind of artist and poser, coked-up gallery owners mixing it up with the critics, everyone with an eye on the door to see who would come in next. The atmosphere, as someone said, was vexed.
　　Floss was working the room, handing out cards, and shaking hands. She had on a tight brown-pinstripe suit, some kind of yellow silk slippers with a Chinese pattern. Around her neck was an Egyptian choker large enough to be a brace of some kind. Yeah. And fingerless snakeskin gloves.
　　Entrepreneurial Ms.—artsy, but all business.

She hit all the main predators first then began to work her way down the food chain. I figured she would give up long before she got to us.

But she didn't.

Around midnight, she made her way over to our table and handed us a little pink card that said "Floss" (in Shelley Volante script) and underneath it (in Ariel) "Fine Art." On the back was a street map showing the Brooklyn and Manhattan bridges and the surrounding streets with the gallery marked by a pink teardrop. Underneath it, the address, phone number, and "By appointment only."

We asked her to sit down.

When she asked what kind of work we did, we both told her we were wannabees with nothing to show. We were about as low down in the subterranean art world as you could get. I told her that by day I drove a sandwich wagon and Budsy was an electrician.

"A sangwich wagon," she said, like I had fished from the top hat of language some bunny from her childhood. Her ears stood out from her face. She was suddenly that interested.

When we asked her what kind of gallery she ran, she said she didn't really know yet. She was just starting up. She had bought the place and was looking to build her list.

"Field of dreams shit," I said.

She looked at me long enough to make me blush.

She said she had no formal training but told us she had an eye for what was good or innovative, and that she was a good judge of people.

I told her we had no formal training either and that, up to that time, we hadn't been able to convert any of our installation ideas into actual art. Our problem was finding a space to work in.

We talked about our grand vision: making visible what sits on the edge of peripheral vision, revealing it only to those with eyes to see it.

Conceits with a verbal counterpart: what everyone knew but would not say.

Enabling courageous behaviour by identifying the courageous.

Room-sized conceptions, concoctions, confections.

Experiential installations that required electronics; video, audio, and even holograms.

She asked us to tell her more.

At that stage, Budsy and I had already downed at least six pints a piece, so we poured forth.

She listened. Bought us another round.

Listened some more.

Didn't throw up.

When our bullshit finally ran out, Floss made an offer. She'd let us use her gallery space to make—whatever. She would give us three months rent-free. If she liked what she saw she would (if this didn't take the cake) start building our profiles with the aim of launching us and her gallery out into the art world as a single brand.

I pictured
pom-poms
and a
marching
band.

Third Day

The Apostle John on the Third Day

My inner disposition? A perfect rhyme with driving *mist*. Demons were negotiating a coalition with my psyche. I wasn't feeling the wonder anymore about the way my one hundred and sixty pound body tag-teamed with gravity and machinery to propel my black ass across the less-than-pristine wilderness of Northern Spain. Let me put it this way: I was carrying a load.

Nowhere in the brochures did it tell you how much of the Camino ran parallel to secondary roads that became major highways you either cycled parallel to or on. I'd spun the last few miles on a crumbling asphalt shoulder with transport trucks flying past, buffeting me, whipping the atmosphere into a vortex of dirty droplets.

I was riding inside a Turner painting.

My legs ached only slightly more than my neck. My sweat tasted like salt and diesel, with a hint of coin—blood, maybe—an all-over body stigmata?

I was wilting and needed me a chamber maid, a chamber pot, a pistol with one in the barrel and no empty chamber.

I was looking for excuses to pack it in, dump my bike in the ditch, and hitchhike my way to the nearest town, where I might find a little bodega and get real drunk.

I was half hoping for minor injury, like a grated hamstring or a pressure-fractured metatarsal.

I was saddle-sore. To make matters worse, my guts were bad. The night before, they had served us the hostel staple: rice and beans. It was all they had.

Between indigestion and the hard bed, the snoring Spaniards, the sleepwalking Swiss, the English quietly desperate under their blankets, the Germans shouting in their sleep, and Budsy, bunking across from me and cackling with laughter all night about some incredibly funny dream he was having, how was I supposed to get a wink?

Budsy on Day Three

Where was that insane Mick anyway?

Yesterday, he was bugging me for more draws.

Kept asking me why I didn't want to smoke with him.

"C'mon, mon, just a few crumbs, just anickle bit of the herb, an ickle spliff."

Kept saying we was outlaws, not pilgrims.

Artists, not civilians.

He kept singing Trent Reznor: "What have I become, my sweetest friend? Everyone I know goes away in the end."

So eventually—like he knew I would—I just handed the whole lump of hash over to him. Even gave him the tiny pipe I made from the hotel pen.

Truth was, I didn't like getting high any more. I liked the *idea* of getting high. That was some fucked-up shit.

Something I need to unpack.

The Apostle John Answers His Own Question

There is a Bermuda Triangle between what you think you want and what's good for you. Here be the latitude where common sense falls off the radar and the black box is never found. And why be I talking like a pirate, like Johnny Depp? Wait now, by the gonads of Neptune, here be the reason, personified. Behold the avatar of buccaneering in our time. Becalmed in the centre of our cultural sea change sits a skinny, headband-wearing Keith Richards, on a kitchen chair, working on a new tune.

"Come on in, man," he says, motioning to me with a gnarled hand. "Join the band."

Big silver skull ring flashing in the morning sun.

"Sit down. Take a load off. Want a smoke? Here, take a swallow from this; it'll cure what ails you." He pours something clear from a ruby-red bottle. "Want some Merck? I just got a new bottle from Switzerland. No, I said *Merck*, M-e-r-c-k. Ya, that's it. Mick's not here."

What genius once called Keith Richards a "fool killer"? I think it was that old coyote Sam Shepard. He was saying Keith is that one in a million—the guy with the constitution of an ox. The guy who can do it all and *not* die. The devil hiding in a fox. The rest of us will OD doing half of what he does.

Least that's what I used to think. Now I know better.

Now I know that Keith Richards is, in fact, just a persona. Like Winston Churchill. Old Winston never smoked cigars unless he was going in front of cameras or making public appearances. And I have it on good authority the dude hated bowler hats, too.

And old Keith stopped doing all that bad shit years ago. Sure, he whips out a bottle of Jack when the Stones are announcing their next tour. Sure, he always has a glass of orange soda and vodka when he's with a reporter. But here's the thing: bet if you tasted that drink it'd be 98 percent soda.

He can slur on demand. He's a porfessional act-ah. It's his persona. And that—when you think about it—makes Keith Richards one sinistah SOB.

I used to be one of those fools who couldn't tell the difference. Who literally couldn't tell literally from figuratively.

I was one of those lame motherfuckers who bought the whole outlaw thing.

I was the guy who thought only punk-ass bitches ever said no.

Lucky for me, my constitution saved me. I couldn't handle excess.

Physically,

mentally

or spiritually.

And still, for the longest time, I was down on myself about that.

Hated this weakness.

This thing that always undid me with the brothers. Undermined my street cred.

By my late teens, I was hanging with a semi-hard crew I thought was the real, hard thing. I'm talking about the clan from up around St. George.

Shaolin.

I could be found in their cribs or riding around with them, in and out of the city. Uptown to the clubs or over the bridge to Brooklyn.

Pre-gangsa shit, but gangsta all the same.

And everything be fine.

I had the moves, Snoop Dogg-lean and laid back til someone passed me a jay.

Few hits and I was flat-out Goofy.

Not funny goofy. Disney Goofy. With a side-order of Gumby. I was Goofy, Gumby, and Freakin' Fred Rogers all rolled into one J.

When high, my white side came out. My voice literally changed. I couldn't control it. All of a sudden I'm talkin' like Arthur, the little fucking aardvark from PBS who looks nothing like an anteater. And that was on a good day.

Often as not, I'd get the heebie-jeebies, too. Paranoid as a brother dumped out of a car in the middle of Bensonhurst. Be seeing shit out the corner of my eye. Be thinking everyone was laughing behind my back. Pretty soon they were. Right under my nose. Pretty soon, they were lighting me up just to see me blow up. Worst thing was? I tried to play along.

Dumb-ass that I was.

That shit does real damage to one's self-esteem.

Pretty soon, I was nothing to myself.

So I slunk back to New Dorp to spend my days in my bedroom. Started reading. Started to avail of the local library. Loved me the 700s in that Dewey Decimal system. That would be "The Arts" for you ignant motherfuckers.

So many people go wrong when they buy into ideas they have no business buying into. But getting it wrong is what makes you grow. Least that's what Floss says. She says real growth is painful. Says what you don't see when you look at a great piece of art or read a great book are all the veins and tissue still attached. Real artists incubate, gestate, grow the work inside. She told me most of us are carrying these forms around inside us for years until the time comes to bring them out into the light. She says the urge to make isn't some idea—some act of will—it's a physical urge the artist has to obey.

Like taking a dump, throwing up, eating, or being horny.

It's that natural. Only it isn't natural, either.

Body pain is grafted to ideas.

Blood and other fluids mix with market differential.

"Show me a Francis Bacon and I'll show you a lump of red raw liver with the bile ducts still pumping," Floss said.

She said the same visceral laws apply to conceptual art. But I wasn't so sure about that. It being so cerebral and all. The brain is dry. It doesn't cry.

Truth was, what she said made me feel bad because my making never came with any physical pain. I got into installations because no one liked my drawing.

See? Here we go again.

Lately, I've been feeling hijacked by another idea.

Like I might not be a real artist.

For a long time, there was the pure excitement and madness of hanging with Budsy. Of learning a new way to think about art. Then Floss came into the picture and our whole small scene got all infused with love, a rosy globe, a waking dream. And the dream was made flesh. Something pre-ordained.

Next thing, Floss offered us the gallery space.

We mounted a show

Now hey, there's Budsy in the *New York Times*.

Then another show.

New artists came on board.

Then all of a sudden it's the NIGHT of NIGHTS.

The show of shows.

MiCS.

The Man in the Cream Suit walking in. The smell of money trailing him, clinging to his clothes, like he just smoked a hundred dollar blunt.

The man who held the art world in the palm of his hand.

That infection.

Who was MiCS, after all?

Another Keith Richards.

Word.

Floss on the Third Day: Sacred Filth

Floss hardly spoke at breakfast that third morning. She hissed at Budsy, told him she needed time alone. Said she had to "mentally prepare" for the ride ahead, a long climb through hills where the Holy Grail was apparently hidden. Budsy told her to keep an eye out for the grail when she ducked behind the bushes for a slash. Yo, here's one you won't find in the tourist guides: behind every stone wall, in every shady grove, in every hollow and depression along the pilgrim's path, there's an array of turds, images of which, stitched together, would make for a time-lapse essay on decay and fertilization, from the slick, fountain-pen steamer to the mouldy, bone-dry mummy's finger, while the once-delicate (if blighted) tissue roses are reduced by the same time-lapse process to patches of mealy grey, like lichen.

Floss did not find the Holy Grail that day, but she did receive a messenger. While Floss squatted in a thicket of thorns, a woman in traditional African dress appeared at her side.

Floss smiled. "Hiyadoin?"

The woman said something in response. Floss couldn't quite make it out.

"Speak louder," she wanted to say, but she didn't. She was getting self-conscious that the Europeans found her New York manners a bit on the rough side.

The woman's lips moved again. A twitter of sibilance. Floss heard something that sounded like Latin—she heard the word Christus. Maybe not Latin—Aramaic? Armenian? Could it get any weirder out here? Some black woman talking in church language and Floss with her ass hanging out?

Turned out the woman was saying "pissing." It was the last word in a phrase she kept saying over and over and it split with a whistle on her white-white incisors. "Greetings for pissing. Greetings for pissing, madam." And then that was exactly what she did. She squatted next to Floss and released a steaming jet that—according to Floss—struck a gurgling bass note as it sunk into the saturated earth.

"What did you do?" Budsy was laughing.

Floss laughed, too. "I laughed, of course. What else could I do?"

What she didn't say was that, when Our Lady of Lagos departed from the thornbush that morning, she took Floss's depression with her. Something about the exchange lifted Floss's mood or maybe it just coincided with a lift in her mood that was coming already. Either way, the pissing woman and the lighter spirits were linked in Floss's mind.

Floss said she wasn't going to be blue.

Since our first day on the road, Floss said she'd felt under pressure. Sure, it was the weather. Fatigue didn't help. There was the change in scene, the gearing down from the pace of New York life. Not to mention the three-bar evangelical heat radiating from the pilgrims. But more than all of these, what was eating Floss was the idea of pilgrimage.

Everywhere along the route were small cairns with fresh flowers laid on them, memorials to those who'd died along the way. She found herself seduced by the thought of a Camino haunted by the souls of everyone who had walked it from medieval times to the present.

A French priest in Santiago told her that the Camino had a counterpart in the stars, that it roughly followed the Milky Way. But, he said, it also has a counterpart within, a dark galaxy of pain and hurt (even priests were reluctant to use the word sin anymore) that must be encountered and meditated upon if the pilgrimage was going to be a success.

French baloney, thought Floss.

And yet. And yet?

Released from the craziness of her life in New York she did not feel light, she felt heavy.

With no distractions, with nothing to do but cycle all day, she felt the gravitational pull of another life, a parallel life, or parallel lives.

Floss at the Top of Monte Irago

Floss's good mood ascended to euphoria when she broke through low clouds into the clear blue, an environmental change equivalent to a pill that instantly cured a mental disorder years of psychotherapy had only fuelled.

Sunshine! Alleluia! Groups of pilgrims greeted her with cheers, like she'd just finished a difficult stage in the Tour de France. They all seemed awfully pleased with themselves, like they were personally responsible for the altitude.

Floss wondered why they had gathered at the top of this barren hill. On a good day, there must have been a view. Not today. Fifty feet below, the valley was a trough of dirty wool.

Floss pedalled on, arriving soon after at a mound of gravel with a telephone pole on the top. But the pole had no wires connecting it to any other structures nearby. She slammed on her back brakes, turned the front tire sharply, cutting a scimitar through the gravel.

"Bonjour," an old man in shorts and a Barcelona soccer jersey called out.

"Hello-bonjour."

"Bienvenue à Monte Irago, et La Cruz de Ferro."

Floss looked up and noticed the small metal cross mounted at the top of the pole.

The man was all smiles. He was carrying the staff and a backpack that signified "the walker." The walkers. Everything was different for them. Yes, the walkers were special, a breed apart. They talked about taking this pilgrimage on foot in vaguely mystical terms, where *vague* and *mystical* could be understood as synonymous.

After so many days on the road, it just becomes the road.

There are times I feel as though I am walking in the stars.

My every footstep becomes a prayer.

I am attentive to the natural world around me, to every twig and leaf, every insect, every hair on every dog.

Floss had little time for such delusional nonsense. What the walkers really meant was that, after three weeks of hiking, they had finally moved from their brain's cluttered apartments into their bodies' spacious villas. They were now in shape, or at least in better shape than they had ever been in their lives. They were no longer desk automatons, electronic mosquitoes siphoning junk information through an ethernet connection. They had become happy nomads, falling into loose alliances as they followed their seasonal rounds. And now, with most of the journey behind them, they'd reached their happy place. And after a few more days on the road, they'd reach Santiago, and with that would come a sense of achievement that would stay with them for the rest of their lives. So close they could taste it. Forgotten was the existential despair that had dogged them for the first few hundred miles. Exercise had rejigged the mind/body balance, tipping it back in favour of muscle wisdom. Anxiety disappeared. They were happy to be alive.

So it was from deep inside this pocket of non-thinking that the Frenchman had greeted her. Monsieur of the all-too-revealing sweats. Monsieur of the pendulous ball sack displayed as he bent over to pick up a pebble. He would have loved to impart to Floss in broken English the insights he'd gained from his personal journey . . . if she'd let him.

But Floss was clutching her gut and nodding vigorously towards the chalet behind the holy mound.

The man waved her on, reading correctly the intestine's lingua franca, her colonic Esperanto.

Budsy Plans a Bushwhack

Budsy had let Floss cycle on ahead, but he was still trying to keep her in view. Later, when he saw her pull off the road, walk down into a ravine—a call of nature, he assumed—he sped ahead, passing her bike where she'd left it—unlocked. The bike girl back in Santiago had warned us all not to do that. There were thieves who worked the Camino looking for unattended bicycles. The organizers even went so far as to hire roaming security, the Bikes Templar, as they were affectionately known.

The ride that morning was steeply uphill (Spain, if you haven't guessed by now, is basically one big mo'fukin' mountain). But something in those hills made Budsy's contrarian nature kick right into gear. The harder he had to push those pedals, the happier he felt. Always self-aware, Budsy knew that part of his good mood stemmed from the fact that Floss and I were both in bad moods. If we had brightened up, he would have darkened. Floss told him his attitude had all the attributes of Post-Colonial Syndrome.

What that meant for the future of Budsy and Floss, as a couple, was hard to fathom.

But Budsy's mind was on more mundane matters that morning. He had an itch to scratch. He wanted sex. And soon. He was a horny toad in the horny season. As he'd have put it, he had a stalk on him that'd put cabbage blooms to shame. So he made a plan. He decided to race ahead and find somewhere to buy a picnic lunch. He would then scout out a place to hide near the trail and bushwhack Floss when she came riding by.

Budsy was in a pastry shop/deli when Floss rode past. The sun was shining and it lit up her mop of blonde curls. She was smiling. Budsy read that as a good omen.

The shopkeeper told him that just up ahead was La Cruz de Ferro. He offered to sell Budsy a flat stone he could write a prayer on. The whole thing apparently came in some kind of kit: a plastic bag with a stone, a sharpie, and a selection of short verses inside. Fifteen fucking euros.

Ten minutes later, Budsy pulled into the layby; he spotted Floss standing near the top of the mound, staring at a telephone pole, her back turned to him. He skirted the pile, tossed a stone on it, and kept going.

As he pulled away, he heard Floss call after him but totally ignored her.

Floss Pretends to Make a Wish

Emerging from the *baño de las mujeres*, Floss picked up two pebbles in the parking lot and walked towards the mound. There were pilgrims everywhere, some kneeling to pray, others squatting to look closely at the things people had left there. Everyone appeared somber and respectful. The tradition, according to the information plaque, was to add to the mound a stone you'd carried with you on your journey, one you'd brought from your home.

The shrine was riddled with all these small, symbolic offerings, many of them water-rolled—beach rocks, river rocks. Some were just pretty pebbles: pink quartz, chunks of basalt shot through with pyrite, white quartz, rubbed-smooth sandstone. Some had names written on them in nail polish or magic marker. Others were inscribed with short poems or prayers: most were in Spanish. Still more were painted a single, solid colour to make them stand out.

Floss walked to the top of the mound and, without ceremony, dropped her two stones, one for each of her parents.

She thought about how she did not mourn them.

Did not even think about them anymore.

How she was slowly letting go of the thought that this was somehow wrong.

That she'd been a bad daughter.

That she was damned because she couldn't love.

How her whole life was a sad country song.

Also tugging at her mind was the symbolism of dropping two stones for someone who had undergone her transition. Two more things she didn't miss. Though sometimes, when she squatted naked, she imagined she could still feel them. Ghost balls—a phenomenon well-documented in the literature.

Not for the first time, Floss wished she could be more serious or that she could take seriously the kinds of things that other people took seriously.

In addition to the pebbles and rocks, people had left all kinds of mementos. Pieces of clothing, ribbons, medals, flowers, and what looked to be letters inside plastic bags. There was even a bottle filled with small bones—someone's cat maybe.

On the pole itself people had pinned photographs. Here was a small girl with braided hair, gaps in her teeth. Very obviously sick. There, an old lady in a hospital bed. Very obviously dying.

Someone had nailed a red-and-green baby shoe to the pole. Floss was contemplating this, its Christian symbolism, the violence of it, when Budsy came speeding up the road. He slowed down just enough to accurately flip a flat stone onto the pile before racing off again.

She called out to him, but he didn't seem to hear her. He probably had earphones in.

Descending, Floss searched around until she saw a flat, palm-sized stone—the kind you would skim across the surface of a pond—with Budsy's crabbed handwriting on it, the arrangement of the words indicating a verse of some kind. She picked it up and read:

A cautious young monk, name of Linus,
Thought it sinful to clean out his sinus,
Until he blew a great clot
Of mucous and snot
In the shape of St. Thomas Aquinas.

Landscape with Fox

Budsy raced ahead, standing up and pumping the pedals until his out-of-sync heart told his brain to think he was on the verge of a coronary episode. He thought about the medical he had before getting his green card, the x-ray showing an enlarged heart. It turned out to be a false alarm, a fault with the image. Still, the news stayed news with him, a foreshadowing of some future diagnosis, a terminal sentence to be delivered in a wood-panelled office by a pimple-face doctor.

So he coasted for a while. He began to calm down, look outward again. The landscape had changed. He was in high country now, on a plateau of some kind.. There were suddenly no trees. The vegetation had changed—more thorn bushes, grasses, and low shrubs. He could see a long way in every direction. No privacy. Nowhere to hide up here.

But just then, as if it were the answer to a novena some great aunt had said for him that very morning in the damp stone church of a rural parish a thousand miles away, a fox popped out of the earth about fifty yards from the road.

"*Ola, Señor Zorro.*"

The fox looked at Budsy, raised one paw, and gave him the Vulcan split-digit salute.

OK. That was just me fuckin' with ya—come on now. The hash wasn't that good.

The fox swivelled, scuttled away, stopping briefly to look back just before he disappeared into what must have been one very cleverly concealed den.

Budsy got off the bike and walked across the rattling grass to the place where the animal had been moments before. Sure enough, the ground gave way, opening into a crater about twenty feet across and six feet deep. It was, Budsy thought:

a) a prehistoric house pit;

b) the place where a flying saucer landed; or

c) an old firing range where Franco tested artillery he got from the Nazis.

The ground was dry. Grass crunched underfoot. He looked around for human bones and shards of metal, but found neither. Small white flowers bloomed all along the crater's slope, and Budsy knew at once that this was a fairy place. A hawthorn or a great oak tree had once grown here, he figured, but had been uprooted by a spiritually impoverished people.

It was the perfect spot for what he had in mind.

He walked back to the road, grabbed his bike, and wheeled it across the field down into the crater. There, he spread out a blanket and arranged the food and wine he had brought.

Then he lay in wait, his head just above the level of the trench.

Lying in Wait

From his vantage point in the crater, Budsy spied a pilgrim passing solo, a woman. She was weeping. Bubbling sobs interrupted by angry words she spat in a language that sounded Scandinavian.

That's it, girl, he thought, let it all out.

She swiped at roadside grasses with her staff. She picked up a stone and tried to hit it with her staff, baseball style, out into the wilderness.

Strike one.

Strike two.

She screamed in frustration.

Double Fantasy

A few minutes later, Floss approached from the other direction.

Budsy stood up. "Come and see what I found. Bring your bike."

"Ahhhh, sweetheart!" she said, as she came to the edge of the incline and saw the picnic laid out below. "Ah, hon. Oh my God, this is so *pretty*. And look at those flowers. I think maybe this place is enchanted."

She kissed him.

Next thing, Budsy was on his back, pants open, grass stalks pricking his lower lumbar. Floss straddled him and they kissed for a long time under the Spanish sun.

"I love you," she said.

"I love you, too."

She was still wearing her rain poncho. It covered them both like a pup tent. Floss didn't really like getting naked in front of Budsy. It didn't matter how much he told her her body was beautiful, how long he lingered over it, kissing all the old parts and the new parts, especially the new parts.

Something about being seen naked just did not feel comfortable; it made her shy. She sometimes thought it was because she had once lived as a male and so had not quite fully adapted to having her body objectified.

Her hair lit from behind was like ripe Castilian wheat. "Your hair is like ripe Castilian wheat," Budsy said.

"You're so corny and sweet," she said, reaching down to guide him inside her.

She bore down, then stopped. "Better wait a minute."

He reached for her breasts, letting his hands run along her ribs. She flinched.

"What is it?" He lifted up her underclothes to see.

The left side of her body, along her ribs, was all bruised. Yellow-purple.

"Oh that ... I wiped out the first morning. My bike tire caught a rut and next thing I was in the ditch."

"But why didn't you say?"

"I was too embarrassed. Have to keep up with the guys, you know?"

Budsy knew she was lying. This was no two-day-old bruising. This was more like two-week-old bruising.

"Let's try that again," she said, changing the subject back to the matter at hand.

It didn't go any better the second time.

"I'm sorry," she said. "I didn't bring the dilators with me to Montreal. Things have started tightening up."

"No worries. Here. I have an idea. Let's toss off together. I'll race you."

And so they did, lying side-by-side under the October sun, hands furiously working, occasionally glancing sideways to take in the comic spectacle of the other and laugh.

Budsy won easily. Bolting forward like a sprinter at the winning tape just over one minute later, he deposited his genetic inheritance into the soil of northern Spain.

"El Seed," she said, frowning, while furiously working her furrow.

Then she closed her eyes, stiffened, and cried out.

Budsy knew she was faking it. She knew that he knew.

In the moment, it seemed like the right kind of intimacy.

Floss Explains Budsy's Dream

A little while later, I made my way along the same lonely stretch of the Camino. I was bored, belting out a version of *Ol' Man River* that was half rap and half beatbox. I was really getting into it when Budsy gophered out of the ground and signalled for me to come over.

"What a cunning little love nest for two," I said, settling in, lying back against the sun-warmed grass. There was a sex smell in the air but I didn't comment.

"Here, have a sangwich," Floss said. "Some wine?"

"Don't mind if I do."

"Have any of you been having weird dreams?" Budsy asked.

"Some," Floss said.

"Not this brother," I said. "I been too tired to dream the last couple of nights. Or at least too tired to remember."

"Last night," Budsy said, "I dreamed I ran off the road on my bike and crashed into some bushes. When I came back out, I was completely covered in burrs. I stood by the side of the road, my arms outstretched, while you and John picked them all off me. I can still hear the ripping noise they made as they came off my clothes."

I laughed.

"Hello?" said Floss. "Earth to Budsy? Remember the story of St. James? How he rode his horse into the sea to save someone and when he came out his horse was all covered in scallop shells? And we are talking the Atlantic Ocean here. It's cold. Like brrrrrr?"

"Oh shit. I see it now." He said. "Fuck me. That's rich."

"Or that ripping noise coulda just been the sound of all those farts," I offered. "The hostel was freakin' ripe last night."

Fourth Day

The Apostle John on the Fourth Day: Sucking Fumes

At 3:08 that morning a man started crying, calling out names in German. Two frauleins tried to comfort him. I listened, let his sobs wash over me, bout after bout of snotty, wheezy eruptions, hacking intakes of breath.

Roiling in my hot bunk rotisserie, I counted backward from one hundred for the third time. His outburst—annoying at first—started having an effect on me. Like his tears were some kind of weak acid eating away my crust of indifference.

I started feeling soggy, like a microwaved pancake.

I started feeling panic.

I started feeling as if an invisible hand had reached into my brain and cracked the shell of my ego.

I stopped looking down my un-African-American nose at the world.

I stopped feeling superior to this man—this poor soul I'd only minutes before catalogued as the Berlin Bawler, the Dresden Drooler, the Wolfsburg Weeper.

For a few minutes, I found myself in the firm grip of some kind of religious fervour. God was holding his mirror up to me—telling me I was no better than the evangelical Christians who took shifts carrying a cross the whole eight hundred kilometres of the Camino, who stopped every day to pray and contemplate and sing hymns. He was telling me I was on par with the Japanese

on the tour bus. No better than the man from Mumbai who had
some servant carrying his backpack. The inference being that I
was no more self-aware than the selfish young people out to find
themselves on the Camino. I was cut from the same cloth as Floss
and Budsy with their relentless irony and sarcasm.

It was time for me to open up to the world again.

How had I gotten so closed?

We were coming up to the halfway point in life and, for the
first time, getting a real sense of how hard it was, how cruel. No
matter how you slice it, no matter how thick and gilt-framed your
rose-coloured glasses, the outcome is always the same: we all lose
in the end. Leonard Cohen said it right: "You win a while and
then it's done, your little winning streak."

It was one thing to know it; it was another thing to *know* it.

It was enough to make your heart break.

We need to help each another.

Love, not hate, brothers and sisters.

Tolerance, not ridicule.

Who Did We Think We Were?

I pedalled serpentine along the dirt track and thought about my
friends.

So much of what brought us together had been based on the
idea of opposition.

We were subversives.

Resisters.

Revolutionaries without a cause.

How we didn't fit in

was all we had in common.

Mote, the Apostle John Sings El Blues de La Meseta

I was not, nor had I ever been, nor would I ever be **BLACK ENOUGH** for America.

I look in the mirror and I see light skin, features as Caucasian as African. The only time that changes is when I'm in a club and the faces around me are white faces with freckles. *Then* I feel black.

I'm so white I can't even make fun of my darker brothers—string beans from the Sudan and Ethiopia. It's not that they make me feel inferior. I'm so far away from them on the pigmentation spectrum, it's practically a difference in *kind*.

Confession: my Y membership gives me access to a tanning booth in winter.

When it comes to sneakers, I have a hard-on for the cheap kind; the kind that look like red Converse but are not, in fact, the authentic brand—I like the knock-offs you can get on any street corner. "Y'all, counterfeit kicks is the reason the sisters won't date you." That's what the brothers say.

When it comes to dating, I go with the white girls who want me because I'm a white black man. I'm a semi-demi thrill for them. Negro chorizo. I'm a safe threat. I don't even really dig white girls. Except for maybe Floss. And that's only because she reminds me of Carmela Soprano, star of the number one TV show of all time. Better than *Roots*. Better than any of the movies: *Cry Freedom, Do the Right Thing, 12 Years a Slave*.

The chicks who really do it for me are those South Asians, those bangle-wearing babes whose coppery skin seems to glow from the inside; those bejewelled Maharanis with the high, scolding voices. If only family weren't so important to them. Two dates and they want to meet my mummy, taste her home cooking.

My Ma's no African-American queen. She's as Irish as the day she got off the boat. Wears a headscarf. Tramps through the Pathmark in rubber boots she calls wellies.

For the first ten years of my life, the only black folks I knew were the Jeffersons. Maybe that explains why I can't stand those Nation of Islam names: Shaniqua, LaVernius, Condoleeza, Tyreke, or Javon. I slam that shit.

And I hate the brassy mouth of my generation. I know I'm discriminated against—cops be shooting us down like we be coyotes—but I don't use that as an excuse to shout: brothers be against this and brothers be down with that. That shit's fake. Same with the sisters shaking they heads, wagging fingers, talk to the hand. You can say it's just style, but style is the avatar of substance. Word.

So I'm a throwback to a bygone era. I'm a reserved black man. I'm a Sidney, a Benson. I'm a Duke, a Nat King Cole.

I'm Barack Obama. But lighter.

Back in my "Young, Gifted, and Black" phase, I tried to grow an afro. I thought I was the shit with my nappy head, my Adidas tracksuit. But everyone said I looked like Richard Simmons. Not fit. I still don't fit.

So goes my catalogue of self-hate.

The Apostle John Experiences a Chain Drain

Chain crunch, rattle-snag on the cogset. Shit. Motherfucker and shit.

"Chain's off," I shouted to the others, told them to keep going, told them I'd catch up.

Getting the chain back on was usually a one-minute job. I'd done it so many times I had a grease monkey's hands. But this time it was all snarled up in the rear derailleur, like one link had kinked, buckling the chain back on itself. Took me ten minutes poking at it with a stick to get it loose.

Back on the road again, riding the dusty shoulder, I'd gone no more than a hundred yards when my legs suddenly stroked out, began to turn so cartoon-quick I knocked my left knee hard against the bike frame. Knee-knock nausea. For a second I thought I'd upchuck.

Motherfucker.

Recovering, I had time to process the sound I heard a split second after the tension went out of the pedals, a splat like someone had flicked a full Venti latte into the dirt just behind me. I looked back to see the chain lying on the ground: Staff of Asclepius between the intertwined tire-tracks. Fuck.

I poked around in the beige dust to see if I could find the broken link's outer plate, the little metal bit that looks like the Lone Ranger's mask. I thought I might be able to snap it back on if I could find it. No such luck. I pulled out my phone.

No bars. I picked up the chain and put it in my saddlebag.

I was going to start walking,

but then I started thinking.

The Apostle John's Buffalo Mozzarella Vision

Dope gets you through times of no bicycle chain better than a bicycle chain gets you through times of no dope, I decided, adapting the old Freak Brothers adage to my situation. I always loved those hippie comics—like the one where Fat Freddy demonstrates his cat's intelligence by picking it up by the scruff of the neck and asking "Who's the Chairman of the Peoples' Republic of China?" He yanks the cat's tail, hard, until it howls, "Mao." Gets me every time.

So I remembered that one joint I'd saved from Budsy's grabbing hands and lit that little number for myself by the side of the road. I was chill. I was cool. Racing ahead only made me a fool. Like whitey. Lord almighty.

Pretty soon, there was no place else I wanted to be except sitting by the side of the road in Castile, watching the breeze bend the tall grass, listening to some invisible bird singing its feathery little ass off high above me.

The sky was the colour of a 1970s wedding suit, powder blue.

The clouds were ruffles.

The wheat had been harvested, the stalks ploughed back into the fields.

The air was silky and pleasantly cool.

I rapped to myself like a fool.

A minute passed, or twenty minutes passed.

Sometime in that interval I had a daydream. Not the kind where the heavens part and God or one of his Netherland Security Angels appear. More like I'd been bit by a burrowing insect of the invisible. An aura-tic. As if the nowhere that fed my life in mysterious ways had sent an emissary to tax my blood, but just a jot.

I was a baby on my mother's lap, only I was not a baby but a round roll of Buffalo Mozzarella cheese, soft and creamy, with big, blue-tinged, rubbery lips. I was sucking on my momma's Irish titty, which was as plump and white as I was, and full of the sweetest milk. I was on cloud nine. I was made out of the stuff I was drinking. I was pure.

And this was probably heaven.

But then I saw where life had brought me.

To the Castilian plain,

to the high Meseta,
where exhaustion passed through me like a blade.

I saw in my transected being that I was shot through with black dots and that some of them had dilated, like spots of mould. I knew this was experience. These were the hurts that didn't heal, that turned to hate.

I saw, too, that there were no great flaws in me. None of that penetration had broken me open, caused me to shatter. I was made of the same pure stuff all the way through. I was better than everything that had corrupted me—the sickness in others and in society—I was not beyond redemption.

I knew then, that even though I loved Budsy and Floss, I was moving away from them. Our lives would have different destinations.

Floss Takes a Detour

When she hit the road that morning, Floss had no idea it would be our last Camino day.

The day was following the usual pattern: we cycled together for a few miles before slowly drifting apart. I was the first one to fall behind—that bran muesli cereal kicked in with a vengeance. Then Budsy got all macho, all mustang, wanted to race Floss. When she said no, he sprinted ahead, said he would wait for her at the next village.

The morning was uneventful for Floss until a minibus packed with hippies, or new age travellers, and piled high on top with camping equipment, almost ran her off the road. They were all belting out a song, like they were on their way to *Camp Winnebago*.

Then, sometime before noon, as she was pushing hard for the summit of a small hill, her ride got bumpy all of a sudden: she could feel the stones on the road, like she was walking in thin-soled shoes, the kind you get two pair for five bucks at Payless. By the time she got off her bike, its back tire was not so much a tube as it was a ribbon. A rubber stocking.

She put her bike down on the road and unsnapped the pump from the seat tube—for you pedestrians, that's the side of the inverted triangular bike frame nearest the back wheel. She attached the pump adapter to the tire valve and pumped hard for a minute, then stopped to listen. Even with the sound of the shaking roadside grass, she could hear the hiss of air escaping.

A puncture.

Floss had been waiting for this to happen. She was almost happy about it—a can-do challenge for Frontier Floss. Bring it on. In the old days, you had a shit-ton of excuses for not knowing how to fix anything. Manuals were hard to come by; repairmen were a dime a dozen; and there were fix-it shops on every block. You didn't throw out your vacuum cleaner when it lost its suck; you didn't throw out your toaster when something pinged and the red arc of an element had cooled to two ash-grey sutures. Irony of ironies that now, in an age when everything is made to be disposable, when if it breaks, you throw it out and get yourself a new one, that in this time of waste, the do-it-yourself tutorial is so easy to find. You're always a few clicks away from laying hardwood, installing doors, or wiring a new motor into your washing machine. It's all out there: discoverable on video, in colour and in HD, and, surprises of surprises, most of it is easy. Like everything mechanical it's all a process. It's all doable if you follow the steps. Thanks to the internet, expertise is on the endangered list.

Floss unstrapped the saddle bags and flipped the bike upside down, balancing it on its handlebars and seat. She removed the patch kit from the tool pouch under the saddle (the bike scrotum, as Budsy called it). The kit contained all the necessary pieces: universal wrench, tube of glue, sandpaper, and patches. Floss mentally replayed the YouTube puncture-repair tutorial she'd watched four times on her phone in Dublin Airport. She was going with the advanced method: how to find the puncture without using water.

She scooped the tire off the rim and let it fall to one side. She pumped the tube until it looked like a black balloon a clown might twist into a puppy at a kid's birthday party. A mini Jeff Koons in matte finish. She inspected it, inch-by-inch, her face so close she felt the air escaping—an invisible, ticklish stalk. When she spat on that part of the tube—bingo! Little blisters animated the smear.

She dried the area around the puncture, buffing it with a tiny square of sandpaper. She put glue on the cherry-red repair patch and stuck it on. Then she lit a cigarette and waited for the adhesive to harden. Five minutes, the instructions said.

She watched as a trickle of black ants started exploring her saddlebags.

Time up. She eagerly pumped up the patched tube. It seemed to hold. But no. It was going soft. She could feel it flutter. And then Floss felt sympathy for men the world over who suffered from erectile dysfunction. No doubt about it, there were more punctures. If she was going to find them all, she would need water.

Floss Encounters the Landscape

Floss kicked through the undergrowth, following the down-slope from the road. Small moths flew up around her feet, flitted and swerved in a way that made her think of electrons. The lay of the land was curved in such a way that only a few hundred yards from the road, she could no longer see it. Just a high ridge and the tops of telephone poles. The earth was soft, and the wheat stalk— some of it already decaying—gave off a sweet smell—like nut paste on warm toast. Open fields made Floss very uneasy. Finding herself in an empty landscape without a building in sight was like encountering some new branch of science she knew nothing about. In New York, she avoided parks unless there were lots of people around. Grassy or bushy areas in the landscape were as irritating to her as unwanted body hair. Who knew what was hiding in there? To Floss, open space felt loaded with eyes—like some legion of pervs was watching her through high-powered binoculars. Who would hear her scream? Cows? Sheep? As if any of those slack-jawed creatures, destined for freezer bags themselves, would ever lift a hoof or a paw to stop some woman from getting butchered.

Floss and the Hare

A hare broke from its cover to her left, loping across her path, watching her out of one terrified eye. The little fellow was right out of *Alice*, though he was not white and he didn't have a pocket watch. Also, he was a hare, not a rabbit. He was brown like everything else. She whistled at him through her teeth and he picked up speed, slowed down, spurted, altered his course a number of times, occasionally took long leaps.

The Incident at the Trough

Floss walked on, coming at last to the green strip she had seen from the road. The meadow was knee-high and consisted of broad, rough-edged grass that left white pre-scratches on her shins. Near the centre of the area was a large and rusted metal trough.

There were no animals—cattle or otherwise—anywhere to be seen, though a patch of cracked, hoof-churned mud bordered the trough on one side.

She expected the interior of this metal bath to be dry, expected to find silt and rust flakes inside. Instead, Floss was pleasantly surprised to discover that one end of the trough contained about eight inches of water.

As she filled her water bottle, she was distracted by a tickle just above her right ankle. She lifted her foot at the same moment the feeling turned painful. She kicked out her leg, hoping to shake off whatever had attacked her.

She sat down on the edge of the trough and rested the afflicted foot on her left knee so she could inspect the injury site.

There was nothing much there. A small red dot—a bite, a sting?

Her thoughts were drilling down into her brain stem. Anxiety splashed up. Could it have been a scorpion? Were there even scorpions in Spain? And if there were, were they the venomous kind? And if poisonous, where did they fit on the LD50 venom test? At the weak end of the spectrum—not much worse than a nettle burn? Or at the other extreme, packing a punch like that of the Australian fierce snake, a single bite from which contains enough toxins to kill over one hundred people, or 250,000 mice?

Get a grip, Floss, she told herself, before ignoring her own advice.

Oh my God. I could die here. Her hand covered her mouth.

A group of crows lifted out of nowhere and began to fly around her, cawing and bickering. She shooed them while trying at the same time to inspect the ground around the tank. She couldn't see any kind of insect: not an ant, not a scorpion.

It was probably a wasp, she thought. It was fall after all. Or maybe she'd disturbed a bumblebee's nest. Was it bees or wasps that could only sting once? She hoped it was wasps. She pictured a windsock-shaped yellow-striped thug curled in fetal position, bleeding from the ass. She wished for him a nice, slow death.

Reunion

By the time Floss got back to the road, I was there, standing next to her upturned bike. "I'm not the only one having trouble," I said, swinging my busted bicycle chain above my head, turning it into a bullroarer.

"Can you fix it?"

"Not unless you have a soldering rod and a blowtorch. How about your puncture?"

"I fixed one hole but there's a second one. I went to get some water to test it. But now I realize I'll need something to put the water in. We have to find something we can submerge the tube in."

"I have it," I said. "I used to do this all the time when I was a kid."

I went to my saddlebag and pulled out an empty plastic water bottle. I took a penknife from my pocket and cut the bottle vertically, and all around, about one centimeter to the right of the neck. "Voila," I said, turning the bottle sideways, "a rat bath."

I laid it in the dirt, filling it with the murky trough water. While I did this, Floss pumped up the tube.

As we were examining the inner tube, a man dressed all in black and walking with a large staff came over the hill.

The Doctor

"Morning."

"Hey," we said in unison.

"Doctor James O'Neill," he said, his voice pinched.

"Howdy, Doctor," I said.

"Hello."

"Hello, James," said Floss.

No answer.

"Hello, James." Floss said again.

"It's Doctor, if you don't mind." He was wild-eyed, unshaven, and looked more than a little acquainted with the demons that come as a package deal with forty days in the desert.

"Whatever."

"It is customary for a physician to be addressed by his title. It is considered a mark of respect. I am a member of the Royal College of Surgeons."

Floss fixed him with a look. This wasn't the first megalomaniac we'd run into on this road. On the second night, we'd been sitting in a cantina outside the hostel when a group of Canadians, led by a Catholic priest, showed up. The kitchen had just stopped serving and the news sent the priest into a rant. What kind of hole-in-the-wall was this? he wanted to know. Who were these people to refuse bread and water to those doing the saviour's work? To those on holy pilgrimage? The guy raved on and on until the cowed waitress went inside and returned with a platter of bread, cheese, and smoked sausage.

The third night, at a different hostel, we were talking to some hostel workers and pilgrims and the subject of the priest's behaviour came up. This kind of thing wasn't unusual one of the employees told us. There was always tension along the Camino between the locals and the pilgrims. A lot of pilgrims demanded special treatment. They thought the local businesses were taking advantage of them. They'd been known to get angry when the path got blocked by herds of sheep or if they had to move out of the way to let a tractor pass. They'd been known to hit passing cars with their walking sticks.

"If that's what you need in order to feel whole," Floss said to the doctor.

"Americans," he intoned.

"Born and raised and proud of it," she answered, surprised by her patriotism.

"Some brand of a feminist, too, I'd say."

"Oh, worse than that," she said. "You'd be shocked, James."

"What do you mean by that?"

Things were escalating. I got to my feet and walked over to the man. "With all due respect, Doctor, we're just trying to fix a punctured tire. We aren't looking for an argument. We've got no problem with you and will be moving along just as soon as we're done."

"Ye should throw those bikes in the ditch and make the pilgrimage on foot. Going by bike only makes a mockery of the good intentions of others. Do you think they went on bicycles back in the days when the Knights Templar protected these roads? In those days they were beset by dangers on all sides. Bears, wolves, wild pigs. Muslims. In the museum in Roncesvalles you'll see a wooden carving of a pilgrim being eaten alive by five or six dogs."

"You have a good day now, Doctor," I said, turning my back on him. I pumped the tire again while the old guy huffed and puffed behind us.

"I mean no harm," he said.

Neither of us said a word.

"Good day to ye, so."

We listened as he walked away. I wiggled my eyebrows at Floss. Then we got back to the job at hand. She steadied the makeshift trough while I passed the inflated tube through the water. Sure enough, we found a second puncture. Then a third. I cut the patch in half and we repaired both holes, only to see the tube deflate a third time.

"I guess that's it," Floss said. "We are both walking. We'll call Budsy when we get a signal."

Budsy on the Fourth Day: the Odour of Sanctity

Pilgrims told us La Meseta was the worst part of the journey, so uninspiring, so monotonous. A few gestured with strained expressions, as if to say it might offer something more than boredom, if not a dark night of the soul then maybe a minor depression?

None mentioned the high plateau, the sweet air, and the white pages of silence. After two days cycling through hilly and mountainous terrain in the rain, Budsy was lifted out of himself by this altitude, by the gymnasium of air all around him.

He could breathe again.

He told us he'd been ill at ease in the mountains—hated the way they loomed. All that airborne tonnage. It was like someone standing over his shoulder, he said. Like Father Bannister, his math teacher back home in Ireland.

"That old torment. He'd walk up and down the aisles between our desks while us boys worked on the math problems he'd set us. We could hear him breathing through his hairy nostrils whenever he stopped to contemplate some poor kid's work. The tension. We could never predict what was coming next: a blunt finger jabbed at some error on the page; a slap across the back of the head; a hand grabbing your neck, lifting you out of your seat; Father Bannister roaring at you to go stand in the hall."

"But why, Father?" we'd ask.

He never explained himself. Just a curt "Don't play the amadán with me."

Budsy told us how sometimes Father Bannister's meaty mitt came to rest on a shoulder, followed by a grunt of approval, or a begrudging word of praise—"good," or "an improvement."

So Budsy learned young how to work the invisible middle ground—the spot where he was least likely to be beaten or praised—the place (he came later to understand) where he contracted his lifelong anxiety.

Folks say you can tell when a saint is near because of the accompanying scent of flowers. Saint Thérèse de Lisieux smelled like roses before her death. That's where she got her name, the Little Flower. The blood that issued through Padre Pio's stigmata was supposed to have smelled like perfume.

The odour of sanctity, it is called.

Modern science has another explanation for the smell: it's what happens after excessive fasting or starvation; it's the scent of the body burning its own fat reserves.

None of the priests who taught Budsy ever gave off any floral bouquet. They smelled of urea, whiskey, mothballs, and sometimes of too much aftershave. The odour of the presbytery was how Budsy thought of it, the smell of excessive loneliness.

On La Meseta, riding across the brown plateau of northern Spain, Budsy shook off such thoughts. Obsession-free for a while, he tasted something sweeter, something other than the self-conscious and bitter stew that was his typical daily contemplation.

Budsy and the Spanish Hare

The hare raced out of the grass just ahead of Budsy, so he hit the bike brakes hard. The hare stopped, too, but the animal stayed cocked, like a sprinter in the blocks. He watched Budsy out of one side of his coconut-shaped head, through one round, brown, unblinking eye.

Budsy and the Irish Hare

Three years earlier, sitting on the tarmac in Dublin Airport waiting for take-off, Budsy had watched a hare watching him from the edge of the runway. Budsy was a little tipsy, 2.75 sheets to the wind from the pints of Beamish he'd downed in the departure lounge. After an hour in line on the tarmac, the alcohol had started to break down, condense in his vitreous humour as he watched the evening fall, the countryside fade, the depth of field shrink to become only what was visible under the airport's orange lights.

Surprising himself, Budsy started to weep like the cistern in a dank public bathroom.

No matter how many times he came and went, the experience of being home always made Swiss cheese of his resolve. Undermined it to the point that he forgot whatever it was he'd promised himself. Some violation of identity happened every time. Budsy had gone against his own grain, not once but twice—once on arrival and again on departure. Each new betrayal built on all the other betrayals he had had heaped on himself from all the years of coming and going.

Home—the word echoed, as though it were some underground chamber, a honeycomb maze or a wasp's nest full of whispers. A prison.

He may have moaned aloud, as he sat in Row 26, Seat D

He was on the edge of an abyss when into the void slipped his favourite grandmother, Granny G, carrying her pisspot—her chamber she called it—a newspaper balanced on top, as she glided across the living room, humming some tune or other. "Excuse me now, I just have to empty this."

Budsy and the Hare Trigger

The Spanish hare started, leaped into cover—brown and fawn fur merging with fawn and brown grass. No sooner had it disappeared than—*Eureka!*—Budsy found the solution to a problem he'd been puzzling over for weeks. He'd been mulling the installation piece MiCS wanted him to do for the grand opening of his house in Dublin.

"It's not what you think," MiCS said. "It will not just be a party. The only other place you will see all these names together is on the advance guest list for the Venice Biennale. The difference here is that *you'll* be the main attraction. You'd be wise to bring your A game."

For weeks, Budsy's idea had hovered in the B+ to A- range. But now he had it. Or at least he thought he did. Rabbit fur was the missing ingredient. That and a single skinned rabbit, boiled. There would have to be steam, a cauldron effect.

He ran over his idea a few times. He couldn't see any flaws.

He felt a surge of excitement at the thought of putting it together, performing it before such an exclusive audience. His ego secreted a hard new layer. Performing at the MiCS mansion was a long way from Budsy's humble beginnings.

Budsy's Humble Beginnings

Budsy looked back from where he'd come. No sign of Floss or me. He was hot and dry. Thirst was he. He had forgotten to fill his water bottle that morning and was sipping on the last stale inch from his previous day's ration. His mind kept running to Finnegan's, his first New York drinking establishment.

It was the favourite watering hole of the Manhattan construction company he worked for. The boss, Joe, ex-pat from Castlebar, in County Mayo ("Eggs and rashers for the Mayo smashers; hay and oats for the Galway goats") took a liking to the lanky Galway redhead and trained him in the installation of Honeybear air-conditioning units, the kind you see pillboxed on skyscraper roofs.

Joe thought the work was rocket science. Budsy, a trained electrician, found it easy, but knew he'd be a fool to set his boss right. The money was good compared to what he would have made back home. And when overtime was thrown in, it was out of sight.

They were working a high-rise job on West 58th Street. Following the usual workday routine of lunchtime beers at Finnegan's followed by Budsy drinking more Buds with his buds after work, also at Finnegan's. Sometimes the after-work sessions turned into evening sessions. Staying late was not a problem for Budsy. He had no social life. And he was easygoing, willing to play along with the blarney, willing to support shamrock visions of the old country while keeping pace with the best of them. He was young. His hangovers were still on the charts.

Mostly, the work crowd was older, married guys. Some nights, the bartender spent half his time fielding calls from their wives and girlfriends. Which was shitty, Budsy thought, though he didn't say it at the time. A couple of the "lads" were from home and had been in New York long enough to be permanently homesick and deep in denial. A few drinks turned them into sad-eyed puppies. But most of the crew were Irish-American or Italian-American.

Budsy got along with everyone. The boss liked his work. Just how much, Budsy didn't realize until near the end of his first summer when Joe sat him down at the end of the bar, said he had a proposition.

"Here," he said, pushing an envelope towards Budsy.

"What's this?"

"Open it and you'll find out."

Budsy opened the envelope and found official papers certifying that he—Brendan Loftus—was officially certified to work on the air-conditioning units he'd been installing all summer. Budsy shot Joe a look.

"Now hear me out. You're a good lad and everyone likes you. After three months, you know more about the electrics in them units than anyone else. Going off to get licensed would be a waste of your time. I know a guy who knows a guy and we came to an arrangement. These are all legit."

"I don't know what to say," Budsy said, "but the thing is, I'm leaving in two weeks."

"Well, here's my proposition," Joe countered. "There aren't many people around with master electrician papers *and* this particular qualification. I can make a case for you getting your green card. All you have to do is fill out the application. Jump through the hoops. You'll have to work illegal until the paperwork comes through. But that's no problem. I'll just pay you under the table."

Budsy didn't have to think too hard about it. The thought of putting his hometown permanently in the rear-view mirror sparked him; the thought of a new life fizzed his central nervous system as if he'd just grabbed live wires in both hands.

He played it cool. "What's the catch?"

"Ah. You're a cute hoor alright. They'll be picking the dead flies off you in no time. There's no catch at all. Except that I want you to commit to working for me for five years."

"Do you want that in writing?"

"Not at all. We only need to shake on it."

"Fair enough." .

A Near Miss for Budsy

A beige minivan sped around the corner. Horn blaring—not so much in warning as in greeting—it roared past Budsy in a cloud of Meseta dust. In his surprise, Budsy forgot to shut his mouth. A stale host settled on his tongue before melting into silt. Grit crunched when he clenched his teeth. His eyelids snagged on his eyeballs and started to burn.

Above the engine's roar, he could hear people singing or chanting.

He watched the van ascend the hill: it had a school of Jesus fish on the back door; its exhaust system was yo-yoing; its roof rack was piled high with backpacks and bags. As it approached the summit, a passenger stuck a tanned and elegantly long arm out the window and waved.

The van dipped out of sight.

When the dust settled back into its bed of dirt, Budsy saw that several sleeping rolls had fallen off the van's roof and landed by the side of the road. A closer look revealed four down-filled bags in slipcases and a sky-blue tarpaulin tied with twine.

All was quiet.

That van was long gone.

And still no sign of Floss or John.

Budsy hooked the sleeping bags to his bike handlebars and made like a refugee for the top of the hill.

Budsy Composes Himself to Wait

He wheeled his bike off the road and leaned it against a granite outcrop. He piled the four rolled sleeping bags against a pile of stones to make a padded backrest. He looked west—back in the direction he'd just travelled. White quartz flecked the steep rock walls where the road cut into the hillside. The landscape was textile art: brown and beige strips, rags sewn together. Following the rule of threes perfectly, two-thirds up the frame was a lush stripe pocked with evergreens—maybe a riverbank—and behind that— a cluster of buildings: pink mud walls and brown tiled roofs. To the left of the houses he saw a church, its spire reaching about an inch into the enormous blue sky. There were no clouds.

An Hour Passed, Followed by Another Hour

13:25 European time. Still no sign of Floss or John. Budsy dug into his saddlebag and pulled out an energy bar: a slab of caramel studded with nuts, seeds, and chocolate chips, like something you might see hung by a birdfeeder, next to the cuttlebone and the suet bag.

He wolfed it and washed it down with his last few drops of lukewarm water.

He thought about Finnegan's again.

The heavy wooden stools. The coolness of the deeply lacquered oak bar under his elbows. The taps and their holy order: Bud, Michelob, Miller, Heineken, Guinness, Harp, and Mickey's Red Irish Ale. Soccer badges behind the counter. GAA county pennants for hurling, and football. Baseball or MLS soccer on the TVs suspended from the ceiling on chains.

For two years, Budsy spent six nights a week in Finnegan's. But that was before the downturn. Before black March, when all the big contracts dried up and blew away. Back then, he knew the pub's schedule like the back of his hand: Jazz Monday. Soul Tuesday. Top-Forty Wednesday. Hip-hop Thursday. Free-for-all Friday. Irish traditional on the weekends with a come-one-come-all session on Saturday afternoon.

The spring-loaded door to the men's had a way of swinging back and smacking you in the shoulder. The underground toilets were unheated and stank of piss and the mineral smell of wet concrete. Green stains down the urinals; "St. Patrick Wuz Here" cut into the plaster above the second one on the right. Condom machine: "She'll love you for wearing one." Missing tiles like missing teeth.

His last six months in Finnegan's, Budsy kept to himself. The crews had gotten smaller as the jobs became fewer. The mood of the place soured. Budsy only turned up two or three nights a week at the most. He was busy. He had other pipes in the fire.

A Cuban guy Budsy sometimes partied with, who lived next door in the same shitty apartment block, introduced him to LSD.

The barn doors of perception undulated open and all the animals limboed loose. Budsy discovered Saatchi Art on the internet. Started going to galleries and museums. Bought subscriptions to *Artforum* and *ArtNews*. At the local branch of the New York Public Library, you'd find him in the 700s instead of the 800s now. Armloads of art books on his coffee table. He started experimenting with LED lights and switches—stuff he could easily take from job sites. He tried working with video, using smartboards as canvas. The stuff he couldn't find out about on YouTube wasn't worth knowing. His mind expanded.

Thursday was LSD night—part of the overall program of self-renovation. If he was getting the heebie-jeebies, Budsy'd hit Finnegans. It was hip-hop night, so the older guys tended to stay away. The music rotation was highly defined. Eamonn, the bartender, played Eminem's *8 Mile* and Head-Butt Clancy's *Don-K* back-to-back, over and over.

> Tonight I just wanna get shitfaced,
> get elephants with Quack Quack,
> get hopped up with Quack Quack and Schlomo,
> clobbered until I yabber in Yiddish,
> poleaxed with Alex and Alix,
> tonight I just wanna get shitfaced
> set my compass for way out-of-bounds,
> be a Titanic that sinks with all hands.

Budsy on LSD in Finnegan's

Budsy sat at the bar, the heavy bass waxing and waning, the walls breathing, the light reminiscent of Van Gogh's *Potato Eaters*, watching his pint of plain settle to black, to cream, the same patented process his dormer went through when dusk papered it, layer on layer, until translucent became a little less translucent, became opaque;

he sat there with doctors, lawyers, bricklayers, and empty nesters, with the children of immigrants, with absent fathers, with the grown children of absent fathers, all those who bore in their hearts the indelible mark of exile, all who knew separateness, who felt cast out, who lived on the plane of voluble sociability, who were driven to ecstasy;

he sat until every syllable in the room became a bubble, and together they made a blonde galaxy, and so sad because he knew that nothing blonde could stay—just ask a comb, just stroll the drug-store aisle of dye—what is light must ascend to the top of the glass as foam, where it must form a diminishing halo, and what is dark must sink slowly into lamentation,

down into the centrifuge of fake grins, red paint, bulging eyes, and harness bells, a vulgar carousel, starting a clockwise spin, like science fiction, like what Allen Ginsberg said about Dylan, how singing made him a rising column,

but what was rising in that room was not just air, but air and water both, a tower of bubbles, its spiral exterior laced with hemp rope ladders, with rungs wide enough for steel toecaps and the reinforced soles of hod-carrying labourers, those who were climbing up, even as they slumped on their stools, or sat in dark nooks sucking sooty thumbs, or wept from loneliness in bathroom stalls, they were climbing up, beginning the hymn, ascending to Eden, rebuilding the wall, the muscle-run-to-flab ex-jocks among them drop-kicking through the goal posts of heaven the rebellious hosts of angels-turned-demons, and seen from a distance, these falling fallen (a numberless multitude) appeared as flecks of coarse black pepper—

a clever illusion, for in truth they were beard clippings culled from the reservoir of an electric shaver that some joker deposited in the stainless-steel canisters that were chained through the centre hole in every refectory table, in the mission where those without any hope of a future were served a message of faith and redemption that was as hard to swallow and as bland as their breakfast, much lauded for its nutrition.

Budsy, the Morning After

"What the fuck was wrong with you last night?" It was Joe, clipboard under his arm, orange-yellow hard hat on (bonjour Monsieur Chanterelle). He was waiting when Budsy got off the service elevator on the 95th floor. "You were above at the bar all night with this goofy grin on your gob. I went up to talk to you but you weren't making any sense. Muttering on about Bob Dylan and the Clancy Brothers. And you kept making like you had a bad taste in your mouth, like you just got a slap of a hot cow shite."

"I must have got a bad pint."

"Bad pint me arse. You were on the drugs."

"Maybe."

"No maybe about it. Listen, you can't be on that sort of stuff and doing this job. Work is getting scarce. We can't afford to fuck up."

He was right. Budsy was always fucked up on post-LSD Free-for-All Fridays. The worst of it was the wire colours—all bled out, the shades all wrong, like in a colourized black-and-white movie. Hard to read the colour codes when they kept changing before his eyes. Sometimes bundled wires roiled like a bucket of earthworms. That was the freakiest. It made him mildly formicate. Then there were the daydreams that could make him laugh out loud or bring tears to his eyes. As long as the drug was in his system, Budsy suffered from poor impulse control. He'd find himself on an empty floor ranting at no one; or, if the acoustics were good, singing.

"Fair enough," Budsy said. "It won't happen again."

"It better not."

Turns out it didn't matter. A month later there were general layoffs in construction and Budsy was among the first to go.

"The residential market is still good. You'll find work there," said Joe.

"What about our five-year deal?" Budsy asked. "I owe you another three and a bit for my green card."

"Well, I can't hold you to it if there's no work now, can I?"

"I suppose not."

"I'll call you back when things pick up."

Budsy knew he wouldn't.

And he didn't.

Night

Floss at Night

Floss was lying flat on her back, looking down on her bug bite: it was now a black-topped red lump, about the size of a cherry, the southwest corner of which showed signs of sending out a spire.

The little church of her infection.

Numbness spread through her body. Where before she could feel every stone, every dip and undulation of the Spanish earth underneath her, she now seemed to float on an invisible cushion of memory foam.

The whole Meseta as yoga mat.

Hi, I'm Matt, and I'll be your yoga instructor.

OK Matt. Let's see your downward dog from behind, boy.

Let's see that junk bump below the rump.

She had a fever. Her thinking was feverish.

What if the redness spread? Where had she read that a blood infection shows as a travelling red line? Had it been in a serious medical journal? (Addiction to health journals is a side effect of gender-reassignment.) Or was it something that popped up on an internet page sidebar? One of a dozen click-bait headlines: TV stars of the seventies: what they look like now; twenty epic costume fails; ten foods to avoid; the fifteen hottest baseball wives; thirty-six ways to lose that belly flab.

We had also polished off several bottles of red wine, some delicious local variety that didn't even bother with a label. And then there was the Spanish cough medicine, *Toseina*, 250 ml, with *Codeina Fofaso*, which we were pretty sure meant codeine. Floss composed a little song in its honour: "Codeina-feena Fofaso: Fee-fi-mo-fasso: Ass-ho!"

The drugs had kicked in—no doubt about it. Floss was no longer freaking out. Silly how she thought it mighta been a scorpion bite. That she was going to die. That we'd wake up in the morning to find her stiff and curled up in her sleeping bag, silvered with frost, dead as a mackerel.

Her sense of imminent death was swept away by feelings of gratitude and amazement. What a place to spend her last few hours! She had never slept out in the open before. The night sky was so full of activity: falling stars, meteors, satellites. Wherever she looked, something *amazing* was happening.

Floss could smell the earth and the grasses. She'd occasionally hear rustling nearby and now and then a sharp cry or squeal. Nature was twenty-four hours. The predator-prey cycle never rested—the Fox Network. But she wasn't afraid. Visions of sharp, feral faces peering through the grass receded. She was beyond imagining a dog's jaws at her throat, its slobber and breath, the cartilaginous crunch of her windpipe collapsing.

At that moment? Floss might've gone so far as to say she was at peace.

The Other Thing that Happened

She was high, of course, bug-eye stoned. Not only was Floss buzzed from drugs and alcohol, she was in the grip of a post-confession endorphin rush that made her feel expansive before making her feel exposed. That's because she'd just done something completely out of character, something she hadn't planned to do, something that only hours before she would have denied she was capable of doing under any circumstance.

Floss had unburdened herself.

This speaking out business had not been scripted. She had no plan. She hadn't been waiting for the right moment. She just opened her mouth to speak and whatever she was gonna say was overtaken. Floss said it was like standing in the ocean facing in to the land and having a big swell lift you and carry you forward with so much power you have time to be both terrified and thrilled before the wave sets you down gently, on your feet, in the shallows.

And afterwards? You can only feel grateful.

She said it felt so good to open her heart to her friends, to elicit the pure attention that is present when people truly listen. Told us she was confirmed in her place by my indignation and by Budsy's anger. Said that afterwards, even as Budsy spooned her, she could feel his brain machinery working. He was throwing off vibes. And at that moment, Floss said, she fell in love with him all over again. Returned to her was the creative Budsy, the guy who made art—not the moody, bumbling fellow who usually floundered through his daily life. Here was the fearless one, the decisive one. The one who saw what needed to be done.

Floss Rewinds to Earlier that Same Day or . . . How Floss Got to Where She Got

It was mid-afternoon by the time we finally caught up with Budsy.

"Water. I need water." His eyes were bloodshot on yellow; pupils like microdots. He had foam and the flotsam of black flecks at the corners of his mouth. There was something pornographic about the movement of his throat as he tipped my water bottle on his head and downed it, making the container gurgle and belch like the water cooler the morning after an office Christmas party.

"Jaysus I was parched. Now let me have a look at those bikes."

Budsy spent a half hour fiddling with my chain and another few minutes studying the valve on Floss's tire tube.

"Nothing for it. Like they say in the horror movies, we'll just have to spend the night here. What do you think? Why not? It'll be an adventure. It's settled then. There's a town about eight miles that way."

"Hey, where did you get those sleeping bags, anyway?" I asked him.

"You're not going to believe it, but they fell off the back of a truck. To be more accurate, they rolled off the top of a van."

"That van jam-packed with Jesus freaks? We saw them. Heard them, too."

"We even have a tarp—it's just down the road there—we can cover ourselves if it rains. Not that it's going to rain. The Weather Network says clear skies and mild temperatures over the next few ways. So will we do it? Have a camp out?"

"I'm game," I said. "But Floss needs some stuff from the drug store—Tylenol, maybe some antiseptic. She picked up a nasty-ass bug bite on her leg."

"Let's have a look at your leg. Oh. Ouchy-ouch. Floss, sure you're OK with a little wilderness adventure tonight?"

"I guess. I could actually use the break from the pilgrims."

"You want me to go for supplies?" I asked.

Budsy stood up. "No man, it's all good. My arse is square from sitting the last three hours."

Floss Fast Forwards, but Not All the Way: Dusk on the Same Day

The next thing Floss remembered was the sound of metal scraping metal. She opened her eyes to Budsy hunkering down in front of a small fire, stirring a pan of beans with a ladle. The fire was made from nothing but brick firelighters. He'd impaled slices of white bread on sticks and set them in a ring around the flames. Reminded her of the pennants landscapers stick in lawns after spraying weed killer.

The light was fading.

Floss was hot, sticky, and uncomfortable. She had drooled a dark spot on her shirt, into the cavity of her collarbone.

Her leg hurt—the bite was now a visible hen's egg under spandex.

"Hey, the dead arose and appeared to many," said Budsy. "I've got your stuff."

He handed Floss a bag containing cough medicine, acetaminophen, and a tube of *crema para después de la mordedura*, more commonly known as *After Bite, The Itch EraserTM*.

"Thanks," she said, rolling up her pant leg.

"Shit, you might want to get that looked at if it's not better by tomorrow."

"*Ola. Ola?*" I shouted into the phone.

"Who's he talking to?" Floss asked.

"The bike people."

I sat down to tell them the news. "The bike guy said he can be here tomorrow morning about eleven. Said he'll try and fix the bikes, but if he can't then he could drive us into their outlet in Burgos and we can get replacements there. No charge to us. Now that's what I call service."

"They probably do this every day," said Budsy.

"How will they know where to find us?" Floss asked.

"GPS coordinates. The phone. It's how they kill terrorists in Afghanistan. The bike guy said he knew exactly where we were. Get this. He said where we are now camped was the site of a famous battle between the Moors and Knights of Castile way back in the way way back. He said they still find pieces of weaponry around here. Floss, you OK?"

Floss felt lightheaded. Her back felt wet. Her armpits were streaming. "Probably just hungry. I haven't eaten a thing since my Rice Krispies for breakfast."

"Food then."

We ate in silence, Budsy crunching on his spoon.

Floss said the beans had a nutty aftertaste she had never noticed before. Maybe Heinz used a different legume in Spain, she offered. The toast was black on one side, doughy on the other, and tasted of paraffin oil. Floss said she would never again eat it any other way. And the wine. It was so light—so cheerful—and had such a surprising finish: raspberries and cinnamon. Floss hogged a whole bottle to herself.

She started to feel better. No less out of it, but better.

She watched the darkness close in, the Meseta shrink to the size of a McMansion living room. She thought of all the people who'd sat around campfires in this place for hundreds of thousands of years, before it was even Spain. Homo erectus, Neanderthals, and then modern humans—she pictured homo sapiens climbing down the ladder from a giant flying saucer, setting out across the high plain, armed with new technology and language— the people who would later become the Romans, the Goths, the Visigoths, the Muslims, the Christians, the Spaniards, the Castilians. Their big brains succeeding through intelligence and a psychopathy that hid behind the golden manifestations of culture: inquisitions, empire, dictatorship. All that shit.

Post-Prandial

"What are you thinking about, John?" Budsy asked me. "You're awful quiet over there."

I was thinking this is the perfect place. We had accidentally found the perfect place for us. But I didn't say so. I was hold-

ing back a wall of bullshit I knew would firehose into the void if I
so much as opened my mouth to speak.

My belly was full—as Budsy would say, hard enough to crack
a flea on my navel. On top of that I was drunk. And icing on the
cake, I was high as well. We all were. We were baked.

My thought at that moment was pressure-packed with enough
pascals to lend conviction to anything I might say. I knew from experience (many wasted hours like this one) that I would speak from
the mountain of my own mind as though it were K2 when in reality (most particularly in that moment) it was a small hill of beans.

Not that this insight offered grip enough to stop the slide.

I was out of control.

God, I was so blasted.

So fucked up that I was burning brain cells trying to parse what cycle of economic corruption had so devalued
the bean that an entire hill was worth less than spit. What or who
had un-jacked them from their GIANT potential?

One thought led to another. I was anchored in the flow, in
the fume of something that didn't so much seem like soul as a
theorem inside which my corporeal being operated. Whoa! And
this thing kept taking flight, blurring off my frame (yea, verily,
as a flame from the wick) cometing into the night sky, whirling
dervishly around the campfire, before roosting inside me again,
drawn back by profundity, i.e., the previously mentioned valua-
tion of that most vital New World commodity, beans.

This was why I didn't say what I wanted to say. Because I
knew that exhaustion in all three of us was a void into which—in
moments such as these—the clichés we had driven out returned
to us from the underworld: refreshed, re-fleshed, red-tongued,
tits-a-twirl, phalluses engorged, glistening gaps agape. Entering
through the gates of ivory (ISP of false dreams) as though they
were the gates of horn (ISP of true dreams).

And we three, we band of boobies, too high, too stupefied
to know the difference, tempted to pour forth barely disguised

exposition, hacking out a narrative of self, before the preacher of ourselves, in the little schoolhouse of ourselves that, in times of extreme inebriation, doubled as a church.

One word, and next thing we would be bearing testimony to our personal manifestos while toasting our toes on the flames. 'Cuz we is artists. Ya, that's right. We be working by different rules. We be a counter-current. We be misfits making a way to fit in. Right on.

I be the black man, but doubly ostracized because—even though I support the aim—I won't play the race game. Won't play the vic-tame.

Word.

Meanwhile, I knew, the joke was on me. I was fooling myself. I was never an artist *by choice*, but because I was LOCKED OUT. The brothers would not let me in. Would not let me be normal. Believe me, I'd tried to blend. If I coulda pulled that off, I wouldn't be here in the dark night where my only companions were white. If I coulda, just one time, looked into my brother's eyes and not seen skepticism, not seen him trying to assess what exactly was *wrong* with this dog. If I had known the secret handshake, the password? I'd be the biggest, blackest motherfucker in the nation. I'd out-Jesse Jesse. Be a bigger hard-on than Louis Farrakhan and the notional Nation of Islam. More cocky than Johnnie Cochran Jr. Gettin' more pussy than Jay-Z.

But say that and the goddamn dam would breach.

Wuh-wuh-wuh, Budsy would chant, pumping his fist in the air. Because he'd be taking me seriously about being the Apostle J, complete with MTV hip-hop intonation and hand gestures: the Slim Shady Chop and the Mos Def Wave.

And this, in turn, would cause him to conflate. Inflate from the same spurious truth-serum injected into his rectum from a beige bicycle pump now extruding from the gates of ivory still masquerading as the gates of horn.

Next thing he'd be the immigrant, huddling and shivering like a bitch in heat, trying to get it on in the New World. He'd be boo-hooing about limited choices: having to play the Mick card, having to jaw with the Tip O'Neill wannabees and the JFKs if he wanted to get ahead.

And as he'd deflate I'd inflate with the same conflation, that gaseous contagion. I'd be just like him. Born in the USA, yes. But always an immigrant. Don't matter how long we been around. Strangers in a familiar land. That's why we be all self-conscious. Why we don't have the confidence of the landed. And so we swagger. We overcompensate.

Then Floss would chime in, say it's the same thing for her trying to fit with that whole transgender thing. And this would likely be where the wheels came off the go-cart.

I know this from experience.

Because either I or Budsy would start telling her that her situation was nothing like ours because the space she was emigrating from—that old binary country—that space was highly defined. But the space she was heading towards—Transland?—that land was Virgin Territory. Which meant her coming out would be clean, and in some ways easier, because said continent was uninhabited.

These were the coordinates where shit would hit the fan.

I foresaw in that stoned moment what would transpire—my prophesy a teabag steeped in the waste waters of the past. Which was why I held my tongue, watched my thoughts arc into the night sky, swift and swallow around the smokeless fire, before flying back into me again.

And still the danger had not passed. I was pulled inexorably toward that sentimental path and would most certainly have stomped down it had Floss not, at that very moment (which may have lasted five seconds or an hour) started to cry.

I had never before her seen her cry.

Her shoulders came up around her ears, her head bobbed up and down between them.

At first I thought she might've been laughing.

I knelt beside her, putting my arms around her shoulders. "Floss? Bae? What is it? What's wrong?"

She forced a smile. "It's OK I'm just feeling weird. I think I have a fever. Or I'm coming down with a cold. Exhausted probably."

I unwrapped one of the sleeping rolls. It was bright green, the fabric quilted like segments on a caterpillar. I placed it on the ground where she could step into it, pulled it up as far as her armpits, and steadied her as she sat down. "There now," I said, I kissed her on one cheek and then the other before I wiped her face with my sleeve.

"You're a doll. And I'm sorry. I don't know what came over me.

"Philosophy and religion," said Budsy.

And again the chasm opened up before us. I frowned at my friend. Floss buried her face in her hands.

"There's a creeping nostalgia to it all."

"What? I heard myself say. I should have ignored him.

"Every now and again I find myself in a pub listening to some old Paddy tellin' his weepy story about the old country, and I start to miss it, too."

There was no going back now. We were being drawn down into the region where self-delusion bloats in the trough of despond.

"Then I meet some old twat who puts it all into perspective again."

"How so?" I asked, firmly grasping this life ring.

"I met this bollocks of a doctor on the road today."

"Doctor James?"

"You met him too?"

"We sure did. He was one badass motherfucker. Came marching over the hill like he was on a mission. Like he was master of the goddamn plantation. Dude almost growled at us for riding bikes. Didn't care much for Americans, neither. At one point I was sure Floss was gonna up and teach him some manners."

"That was probably my fault." Budsy's eyes lit up.

"Why? What did you do?"

"What did I do? Nothing, well—I was standing by the side of the road—leaning on my bike, having a smoke, when along he comes banging his stick on the ground like he's giving the snakes of Spain fair warning. I could tell he was Irish just by looking at him. Big, thick head on him. And the high colour and purple capillaries of a man who likes a drop of the creature. Only in his case, the eyes were crazed and the movements were a bit too twitchy. Like he'd recently sworn off the bottle. I figured he was on a walking cure of some kind."

"Woo-hoo. Listen to you, all Sherlock Holmes. You could tell all that about the old guy from just one glance?"

"Don't get carried away. Characters like him are a dime a dozen where I grew up. So I says good morning and he brightens right up."

"Good day to you, young man. Are you making the pilgrimage?"

"Sort of."

"Where are you from?"

"Galway. Ballinasloe."

"Ah good God above," he says, "I am from Borrisikane meself."

"A Tip man. Lovely country over in Tipperary."

"You don't sound like a Galway man."

"I live in America now. New York."

"And what do you do over there?"

"Sparky."

"You're an electrician. Be-the-hokey you don't look like any working man I've ever met. You look like some kind of an escaped convict with that rig out on you. Ha?" He gave me a bit of a sneer.

"Full marks for observation," I told him, "I used to be an electrician, but I'm an artist now."

"An artist?" He almost spat at me. "Are you having me on?"

"Why would I do that?"

"What kind of an artist are you—a painter? A sculptor?"

"I'm a conceptual artist. I do a lot of work with video."

"Ah. One of those! We have lots of them in Ireland now, too. Pulling on every kind of government scheme and grant. Like a farrow on a sow's teats. Sure that's not art, young man. I suppose you live on hand-outs."

"I don't see how that is any of your business."

"I'm right, so."

"Well, you're not right. I don't live off grants. As a matter of fact, I have a big show coming up in Dublin."

"Oh now aren't you the grand fellow? Big show coming up in Dublin? You're a gas man. A bit full of ourselves, are we?" His face was so close to mine I could smell his breath, like overly ripe bananas. His bottom teeth were clagged.

I asked him why he would ever say such a thing.

"Arry, it's written all over you."

"If there's anyone thinks himself a big shot in this conversation, it's you, " I said. "You're the one pursuing the aggressive line of questioning."

"*Pursuing the aggressive line of questioning.* You sound like a Yank. How long have you been in America?"

"Ten years."

"Is that all?"

"What do you mean?"

"You sound like someone who's been there half your life. Ask yourself this: Why would you be so willing to ditch your own ways and your own people? What are you ashamed of? What do you think they have over in America that we don't have in Ireland? You should be proud of who you are and where you come from. When you meet new people, they should know from the first word that comes out of your mouth that you're a proud Irish man."

"I couldn't give a shite about Ireland."

"Well, now we're getting to it."

"Getting to what?"

And at that point? The wind suddenly went out of him. Like he forgot what he was going to say or had just forgotten himself. Like he'd gone down a path he'd promised himself not to go down again. Like he was making some kind of correction.

"Yeah," Floss said. "He kinda did the same thing with us."

Budsy had more to tell. "So then the doctor says 'You'll have to forgive me. I'm in a bit of a bad way. I used to have a problem with the bottle, so the College sent me to dry out, sent me to counselling, all the usual stuff. The psychiatrist prescribed some kind of mood drug to make me feel calm. To keep my anxiety and depression at bay. But here's the thing. I've discovered that it's an evil pill. In a matter of months, the drugs had completely hollowed out my faith. Jesus, who had always been with me, even at my worst when I drank, was suddenly not there. I looked for him everywhere. But all I felt was a dreadful absence. My life drained of purpose. That is why I'm here. I've walked here from Rome. I'm over five months on the road. I gave up the pills. But I haven't been myself since. I feel like a house with all the windows left open.'"

Floss Cracks

Floss felt strange, unreal, a loose tooth in the gum of reality.

But poetic too, at the same time, all dreamy and floaty—she had to place her hands on the ground to make sure it wasn't about to overturn, toss her to one side.

The sky fell. Diamond-tipped stars piercing her skin.

They were not love arrows.

They were warning shots.

She thought of Saint Sebastian, feather flights, and shafts sticking out of his body. A human pincushion. Paintings always depict Sebastian tied to a tree, slumped in death; but the arrows didn't kill him. He survived. Later, he went to Rome to grieve the matter with the emperor, Diocletian, and got clubbed to death for his troubles. Not the sharpest knife in the drawer, Sebastian.

Floss Confesses

Floss knew this well: to keep quiet was to become a prisoner of memory, was to fatally wound her conscience.

She clutched her legs and started banging her head off her knees.

I sat down next to her. "Floss, honey, what's the matter?"

"He attacked me."

"Who attacked you?" I asked, looking at Budsy.

"He punched me. He kicked me. He threatened to kill me."

"Who did? What the fuck? What happened?"

Budsy and I Circle the Wagons

Budsy knelt in front of Floss, sitting back on his haunches until his face was level with hers. He took her hands in his. "We believe you," he said. "Look at me. Now tell us what happened. We are here for you."

I snuggled in at Floss's left side, putting my arm around her, laying my head on her shoulder. I tried to surround her, cushion her. It was all I could think to do at the time.

But it was Budsy who threw her the lifeline she needed. It came through his unwavering gaze, through an expression that told her, no matter what happened, she'd be OK.

He was a pillar of authority.

In a world of mental eunuchs, this was a man.

I watched her fear dilate and disperse.

Strong detergent on grease.

She began to speak.

Floss: Fight or Flight

So here's the thing: getting beat up is not so bad as you might think.

Of course it depends on the person. If you've never been hit before, it's going to come as a shock. You're going to go into freefall, find yourself on an all-white sound stage where you lose the depth of field. Without your bearings, you'll fall, curl up into a ball, bawl like a baby. Hammers will land on you from every direction. This is what it's like the first time for most people. Even for stand-up guys.

The knack to getting back on your feet is not taking it personal. Weird as that might sound. Hear me out. It's the emotional hurt, the betrayal that's hardest to deal with. The first blows confirm the bad news about yourself: that you are, and always have been, less than nothing.

But once you've been beaten up a few times, you see physical pain as a fork in the road. Two roads diverging in a blood-red wood.

Go one way, you're lost.

Go the other, you're back on home ground.

Floss tried both ways and made the right choice, proving to herself—once and for all—that she had the instincts of a fighter.

That's what MiCS didn't understand the night he laid into her. Before she even crawled into the back of a cab, she'd already started pulling herself back together.

She'd already decided on revenge.

Would the Real MiCS/Floss Please Stand Up

So our man MiCS was the Grand Wizard of the art world. He was Dumbledore and the Dark Lord all rolled into one. The most powerful dealer on the scene, the only broker who could compete with the big institutions. The man who made careers. One snap of his fingers, one nod of his head, and you were in. The value of your work went up tenfold overnight.

Or so goes the myth.

Truth was, out of every fifty artists he gave the nod to, only one would actually make it. And only one in a thousand would rocket into the big leagues.

MiCS was a shark. Had been from the very beginning. Floss knew this—she was not a total blonde.

She knew MiCS had a history of picking up new brands to reinvent his business, to keep it fresh. Made his first money selling works he bought on the cheap from "friends." Moved on from there to flipping blue-chip modern and contemporary work. He was Mr. Capitalism. A demagogue. After the 2008 market crash, he went all conservative, focusing on name brands, work that was recession-proof. Then, when the market roared back to life, he looked around to find out what was new and added conceptual art to his catalogue.

What Floss did not expect was exactly how persuasive he could be, how powerful his attack was, how susceptible she was to that kind of damage. He had such style: the suits, the hair, those elegant hands. The guy was Christopher Walken and Gregory Peck all in one package. And he targetted her personally—Floss a nobody from Huguenot. He knew what she'd been through made her a willy for the big time. He knew she was all wet.

He told her great dealers like her rarely come along.

He said he wanted to do more than just promote her stable of artists; he wanted her to become part of his business.

He made her think he was grooming a successor.

That she would do for his business what Alexander McQueen did for Givenchy.

He told her the dealers were the stars and the artists were dispensable, just moveable pieces in a complex game.

"Gallery owners are matchmakers," he said. "Buyers are suitors. Just because you have the cash to buy doesn't mean you're going to be successful. A good dealer will consider all the factors and will likely entertain several offers before making a decision. It's not just about money. Who collects the artist is important. The right buyer can build an artist's brand. As I said, a good gallery owner is a matchmaker. A bad gallery owner is a pimp."

People whispered warnings, but Floss's ego wouldn't let her listen. The naysayers were all mental midgets, risk-averse small-timers who would never grow beyond their small-market niche.

Was she weak?

She was flattered. It was all so overwhelming.

Walk a mile in her shoes—if you can find them.

A great wave hit the Floss Gallery the night MiCS walked in, and it was thirteen months before her feet ever found the ground again. When you spend that much time chasing the world and the world eventually comes to you? Well, that truly is something—

   why in DUMBO they say

   that Floss's small heart

   grew three sizes that day.

What they neglected to say was that the inverse also happened: the same magic that grew her heart shrunk her brain. Almost overnight, Floss was part of the whole pornographic shit show: auctions in New York, fairs in Basel, London, Singapore, Berlin, the Venice Biennale. Now she gets access to all the studios. Now she only has to pick up the phone, drop the MiCS name, and she's at a private viewing of new works from a major artist or a brilliant up-and comer. Afternoon champagne. Lines of coke if she so much as tapped the side of her petite nose. Artists started getting in touch, offering her work on very favourable terms if she'd agree to represent them.

And we should expect her head not to get turned?

Budsy used to joke that when it came to art, Floss's taste was all in her vagina. What he meant was, Floss used basic instinct to build her list.

Her list wasn't a hodgepodge—she didn't spread her bets. She didn't follow trends. It wasn't about calculating the greatest financial return.

What Floss desired was to feel undressed before a work of art. She wanted the art to erase her shields. If this makes her sound a bit airy-fairy, given to the vapours, a hothouse flower whose judgements were so ethereal she had to look up her ass to find them, it shouldn't. Floss had a killer instinct. She took no prisoners.

The work had to meet her very high critical standards before she'd even consider taking it on. Even then, there was no guarantee.

What she was really after was work that somehow violated her high standards but still lit her up. Work that gave her a flutter under the ribs. Like drinking twenty cups of coffee. Like doing a line of purest blow.

She wanted work that turned the spotlight on her. She wanted the tables turned, to be the one under scrutiny.

The best studio visits stole Floss's sleep, made her restless. Even though the encounter might have been terrifying, Floss knew no other way to build her gallery—a gallery that mattered.

But all this was back when she trusted her judgement completely, before she learned that instinct—like any other faculty—could be corrupted.

"A collection is a personal vision. No one can steal your vision." That line she'd read somewhere became an earworm in the weeks leading up to Floss's big clash with MiCS. It fuelled her growing sense that she was slowly and surely becoming blind. Counterfeit to herself.

At this point, she hardly even felt like a gallery owner.

She felt like a mule. The mule who booked MiCS's appointments, brought him his coffee, dealt with his angry clients and needy artists, the mule who was learning how to anticipate the big man's every want.

And of course, the more she waited on MiCS, the less he gave her in return.

The promises he made to promote her list failed to materialize.

A broken sprinkler head in his Chelsea gallery delayed Budsy's show indefinitely.

Talk of taking Budsy on the road to London and Rome all but dried up. MiCS even started getting irritated when she brought it up. Fucker was fronting the whole time.

After a while, he stopped even paying lip service to her ideas. Soon he was actively ignoring her input. He only responded favourably when she repeated his own ideas back to him.

MiCS wanted a parrot, a mynah bird.
It drove her crazy not to be heard.

The NIGHT of NIGHTS (remix)

MiCS assaulted Floss in the privacy of his Bowery apartment.

It was a Friday night. The two of them had just got back from San Francisco, where a deal to buy a lost Léger had gone south at the last minute.

They were sitting on couches in the sunken part of the room (the cockpit, as it was known) talking business when the discussion got heated and Floss demanded that he live up to his commitments—to Budsy, to the Floss Gallery.

Either do it, she told him, or she was out of his weasel deal.

MiCS had been drinking and probably doing something else, too. He was twitchy and his face had that pulled-tight angular look it got whenever he was exhausted and high.

The death mask.

He stood up, all seven feet of him towering above her, and started yelling.

He called her a tranny cunt. A bridge-and-tunnel girl with delusions. A carpetbagger.

She barely heard him. She remembers a bottle of brandy rolling across the coffee table, spilling amber on the carpet. She wanted to throw a match on it.

He told her he'd had enough of her bullshit; he'd wasted enough time trying to point her in the right direction. He wasn't going to help her anymore. He told her she was too stupid to be taught anything.

"Since you can't learn and you will not take a hint," he said, jabbing his bony index finger in her face, "here's what you *are* going to do."

She looked at her nails.

He told her she would terminate her list, beginning with Budsy. "From now on," he said, "the Floss brand will represent only those artists I choose."

Like she didn't know from nothing.

She said go fuck yourself. Said go fuck yourself with a horse cock. Pulled out her phone and speed-dialled Budsy at their old apartment (Budsy wouldn't stoop at that time to own his own phone—"electronic shackle" he called it.)

It rang once, twice, three times.

MiCS paced in front of her, breathing heavy, growling like there was spittle caught in the back of his throat, a tiny speck of gasoline just waiting for the right spark. The fact that Floss was ignoring him seemed to do the trick.

She was waiting for the machine to kick in when the first blow kicked in instead.

Hard.

His weapon was like some long sock filled with sand or beans, green with black diamonds. It took Floss a second to figure out what it was—the replica cobra he kept coiled in a corner by the door.

The first hit knocked the phone from her hand, nearly broke her fingers. Her mobile skidded across the couch, emitting a tinny beep.

The second blow winded her. She thought her breasts might burst.

She remembered screaming and at the same time feeling embarrassed about the noise she was making.

She remembered his torrent of abuse, the way he swung that snake through the air like he was working a bullwhip, landing blow after blow on her torso and back, then trying to hit her in the genitals.

She was in shock. She curled up, did her best to protect her body.

She slowly regained her senses. He wasn't hitting her head, which meant he was probably not planning to kill her. This beating was his attempt to pacify her. That made her mad. She went into fight mode. And while he exhausted himself battering her body, Floss's mind did battle with her emotions: the shattering feeling that she'd been naïve,

that she'd let herself be taken in,

that she'd let her own vision be compromised by money,

that she'd betrayed her friends,

that the future she'd imagined was gone.

For a while she gave herself leather.

And then she calmed herself.

The blows kept coming, but increasingly they felt distant, like her body was a passenger ferry registering the dull thump of waves against the hull.

Inexplicably, something like joy welled up inside her.

Floss knew she'd won this battle.

She won it the minute MiCS struck the first blow.

He had underestimated her.

Floss had already taken too many hits in her life—literal straight rights and figurative hooks—her identity had already been well and truly shattered, her sense of self was used to a state of flux.

The sutures never quite fused.

She was a puzzle with multiple solutions.

So, even as the last blows fell and MiCS screamed at her to get out, Floss had already reassembled a stronger working version of herself.

Burgos

Driving to Burgos

It was morning—blinding—therefore sunny. I sat up—stiff back—looked up: blue sky pocked with kindergarten clouds. A band of ground mist drifted across the Meseta like an F-16 had sheared below radar, leaving a vapour trail.

A black van was parked by the road. Mountain-bike decals down one side and clamshells painted on each door. A Spaniard in a Manchester United t-shirt and lime Bermuda shorts was standing next to my bike, inspecting the damage to my chain.

Floss and Budsy were nowhere to be seen. Their sleeping bags were puddled, as if they'd been rolled down and turned inside out at the tops to show the white inner lining. The bags were like giant fungi, or some hardy desert plant: its reservoir base awaiting a cloudburst before putting out a long leather stalk where a spiky flower would bloom, but only for one afternoon and only once in a decade.

"*Ola!*" I called to the tour man.

"This one easy." He motioned to the punctured tire. "This one, I not so sure. Maybe I have the piece." He went to the van and rummaged around, whistling a tune I tried to place. It was Simon and Garfunkel's *The Boxer*, only this guy added flourishes the way a flamenco player would add arpeggios to a simple guitar line.

Floss and Budsy appeared then, bashing off one another as they walked, all shoulder and hip bumps, all post-coital grins.

"How's your leg, bae?"

"Much better," she said, rolling up her pants to show a red spot about the size of a quarter. "The swelling's gone down and I don't feel feverish anymore. I actually feel pretty good."

The bike guy came over.

"*Ola*."

"*Ola*."

"*Ola*. This one I fix. This one I no can. Two can ride bikes and one ride with me."

"Can we all ride with you to Burgos?" Floss asked.

The man made a mug and simultaneously shrugged, "Is no problem. There is room."

"Is that OK with you, John? Me and Budsy have decided we've both just about had it with the Camino. Thought we might spend a night or two in Burgos and then change our tickets to fly to Dublin early. We could use some extra time to prepare for the show."

Last Day

We drove in silence the remaining miles to the city of Burgos, a distance that would have taken days by bike.

The subtleties of the landscape faded.

All became flatter and browner, mile after mile.

From the vantage point of a speeding van, the pilgrims, with their sun hats and rain gear, their walking sticks and clamshells, seemed pathetic, anachronistic, a parade of eccentrics and loners, tourists who'd fallen into a trap.

The Camino was just a dirt track by the A-231 motorway, the walking path disappearing as we joined the N-120 at the industrial suburbs of Burgos.

HOWTH

The Biggest House in All of Ireland

He met us—all six-foot-fifteen of the motherfucker—at the front gate, came sauntering down the drive in his cream linen suit, his green linen shirt, his tangerine paisley cravat, the tassels on his boat shoes popping. He threw his arms out in a way that was half gesture of embrace and half shrug. A quarter smile played on the prim mouth that, at birth, had been pulled too far down his droop-eyed, long-nosed, horse face. A forceps delivery.

He's like Virginia Woolf in drag, Budsy said.

When I looked at his hands, at his knuckles, I tried to picture him pulling a Mike Tyson on little Floss. Somehow, I couldn't.

"Howdy," he said, in that accent that seemed to change wherever he went. "Great to see you! So excited for the show on Friday. How are your accommodations? I knew you would want to be in the city. Great. Ya. Great. Would have had you up sooner, but renovations, clients, visitors, a small infestation of wood lice, leaks in two bathrooms. . . So tradesmen, contractors, you know, the whole home-reno shitshow that looks so glamorous on reality TV but in reality is anything but. Let me give you a tour of the place.

You might have heard about the gargantuan success of two Irish developers, Marty Doherty and Finbar Dohey and their company, *MarFin*. Built that famous tower at Canary Wharf? No. Not the one shaped like a rugby ball, the one next to it. Right. Actually, they're responsible for much of the first half of that that whole development. Not to mention their other projects in Dubai and the Emirates.

Their latest venture is social planning. They're looking to give back. They have an idea to redevelop parts of Limerick City, their home town. They say the solution to the gangland warfare there is not social programs, is not youth sponsorship by the Arsenal football team, is not education, is not more missionaries living in Moyross, nor is it more police presence. It's a simple case of urban design. The say their new project, Shambohane, will create not only a pleasant and functional living environment, it will also create a corresponding state of mind, a climate of relaxation and ease. It will make the people of Limerick the most desirable employees in all of Ireland. The mayor of Limerick is totally behind it. The latest is that the government is going to kick in seed money and guarantees.

Anyway, after MarFin made a killing over in London in the 1990s, they were looking to build themselves a home. They could have gone anywhere, really. But you know the Irish. They're like pigeons. Besides, the tax environment was so favourable at the time. So they chose Howth, overlooking beautiful Dublin Bay. In a prophetic move, they bought a very ordinary two-storey, Viking's Elbow (named after a prehistoric find of some kind), on a two-acre site just above the Murky Boathouse. They bought the whole thing for 1.3 million pounds in 1994. Later on, they added a couple more acres and bought the beach rights. They demolished the existing structure and built this 11,000 square-foot, six-bedroom home, with terraced gardens and orangery. Marty has such a green thumb.

So if you look across the bay there, you can see Killiney and Dalkey. The sea view is uninterrupted. And sunshine is assured—when the sun shines—from dawn until dusk because of the southerly aspect. It's an interesting view, too, with a constant armada of container ships and ferries streaming in and out of the bay. Sadly, the ferries are full of émigrés once again. But things will come around. And I suppose it would be hypocritical of me to complain when I got this place for a song.

No, *MarFin* was disbanded after the property crash, but the dynamic duo—while they did have to sell of some assets—didn't face jail time like so many other developers who contributed to the bust. *MarFin* had little to do with the Irish banks. Another feather in their caps, if you ask me.

The property adjoins the former home of the rock star, Nails Murphy, whose untimely death made headlines a few years back. I'm sure you remember.

Yes, you're right, Dublin Bay has been compared to the Bay of Naples. And maybe there is a similarity, but without the pollution, the garbage, the pollution. Not to mention Camorra victims rotting loose from their concrete shoes and washing up onshore.

Down below is the three-bedroom guest cottage. I had planned to have you stay there, but then my sister arrived from France with her three brats. She's going through a divorce. So here we are at the main house. The wrought-iron gates in front of the solid-wood doors are a security feature, but also of some artistic merit. They were made by a local man whose main line of work is making cattle-crushes, believe it or not! The house is Arts & Crafts style, yes, but with something of a New England feel to it. So come in. Come in. Never mind the mess. We're just getting things ready for Friday—

No, that one goes in the second room. See Marcel, HE HAS THE PLAN. (Marcel, my assistant, is the man my sister is divorcing.)

So you might note the unusual layout—the mezzanine level above, for one; that's where I am going to have our guests assemble. Yes, access is by the iron staircases at either end. Budsy, you're going to set up right here, underneath, in the circular foyer. It's going to be fabulous, I'm sure. But why so secretive? No. OK. Artist's prerogative and all that. At least I won't have to *act* surprised. Do you know how hard it's been to get a circular table to your specifications? Counter-high, thirteen feet in diameter and revolving on a lazy-Susan base? We had to have it made.

Anyway, follow me. The layout of this place is quite eccentric: the main receptions flow into each other across the entire main floor, taking full advantage of those waterfront views. It makes for a great entertaining/party room; guests can wander from kitchen to family room to great room to sitting room to dining room to library. And when it's all over, the doors can be pulled across and each room returned to privacy.

Budsy, you'll want to see the kitchen of course. Yes, you can attach the extra gas burners to the main line and run the pipes right out to the foyer. I wish you would tell me more. Insured? Of course I am. Ah, a joke, I see. Funny.

So yes, the orangery—the greenhouse, John, that's right—was added a few years ago. It's the heart of the home, right off the kitchen. I often begin my day here and find that it's evening before I know it. The light is fabulous—especially for studying new works—and the view—well, as you can see—is restorative.

The floors—I'm glad you asked, Budsy—are European oak. Are you serious? Cover them in plastic. You are serious—Gosh. It's going to be that messy? I'll have to... Oh, don't worry about it; I'll have them refinished afterwards. The whole place is being redone anyway. Now that I think about it, they were starting to look shabby. That's the trouble with renovation: the contrast reveals a host of trouble. I'll remove the rugs though—these are Aubussons of antique vintage, eighteenth century. My favourite rug, though, is the Miro in the library. We will get to that.

The décor is restrained, in style with the house. Heated travertine marble floors in the hall and orangery give an almost Moroccan feel on sunny days, even in the winter. Oh dear, I'm starting to sound like some dreadful real estate agent!

But come on. Let's have a look at the Japanese garden. Really, I've had so little to do here. The babbling brook is a joy. Whenever I feel swamped, I just come out here and sit beside it. My muddled mind is soon sluiced clear. I always think of Hercules cleaning out those stables. It's better than an SSRI. The designer—I can't remember his name now—some English horticulturalist—formerly a Trappist monk—sadly ended up taking his own life.

Just over there we have the saltwater pool, the sauna (just the thing for the morning after), and a gym, which I never use and probably will turn into a wine room once my stock is shipped over.

But look, there is one more thing I want to show you—the art up on the mezzanine level. . . This way. Yes, the bannister is bog oak. I've decided to concentrate on contemporary Irish art for the most part. Here, now. Look at this Shinnor. I can't believe a leading Irish critic described those greys as gloomy and sentimental, the artistic equivalent of footsteps in the sand. And this Paul Henry landscape. Actually, living in this space makes me feel like I'm living inside Mr Henry's head. This Ballard nude—well, it will probably turn out to be a good investment. One can hope. I've just decided to move it to the guest house—just now, in fact. Una Sealy, of course, here, the narratives simmering just under the surface. And Robinson. Hmm. Guest house, too, I think.

Hold on now. I have to take this. Giuseppe. Ah, great to hear from you. No. I'm in Dublin. The California piece. He has? Are you serious?

Can you just give me a moment? Sorry, but I have to take this call. I may be a while. Buyer with cold feet.

Marcel! Marcel! Yes, can you take care of my guests. Fix them a drink.

Budsy, Floss, take all the time you need figuring out what you need. Yes, the place will be yours as of Friday morning.

So looking forward to this. Ciao."

The Apostle John and the Blacks of All Ireland

Something about Dublin brought out the brother in me. Didn't take me long to figure out why. The Irish are racists. Two times in two days I was asked what part of Africa I was from. Both times when I pointed out the misconception—while acknowledging the deep connection to the motherland—these whippet-like, track-suit-wearing, suede-head motherfuckers start singing soul classics into my face. *Sexual Healing* and *You Sexy Thing*. And they expected me to sing along. Racist? Not even a little bit. Racist. Racist. Racist.

Weird part was how up-front they were about it. No one stateside would pull that shit unless they were looking for serious trouble. The guy would have to be three times your size, have a posse, or be packing hardware he was planning to use. In Pogue-town, things were different. None of these guys were armed, least not with guns. The vibe was downright loopy. Almost like it was just their way of starting up a conversation. Like they thought they was being the welcome wagon. The upside was that you could tell them to go jump in that smelly fucking river (ripe as Joyce's bum hole) without worrying about them putting a cap in you. Both times when I pushed back they acted surprised and, weird as it may sound, hurt even.

"Why would I want to jump in the Liffey? It's full of shite and condoms and God knows what else."

Both times I found myself almost apologizing. Told them I thought they were fucking with me.

"Why would I be fucking with yiz? Here, let me put you straight, man. Irish people are not like Americans. First of all, we're all white, except Phil Lynott, may he rest in peace. Second, we are not white like Americans are white. We're white like Americans are black. We're the blacks of Europe. And if you're from Dublin and a Northsider, then you're not only the blacks of Dublin but the blacks of all Ireland."

The Blacks of All Ireland struck me as a good title for something

"I know," I said. "I've read my Roddy Doyle."

"Roddy who?"

"Doyle... *The Commitments?*"
"Oh him, Yeagh."

The Apostle John Tugs on His Roots

I walked around the city expecting to feel some kind of connection with the people, the place. My hidden white half was Irish, after all. Nothing—no upswell of sentiment, no jimmy-leg signalling I might break any minute into a Mr. Bojangles jig while crossing O'Connell Street; no glottal convulsions in the form of a brogue. Blame it on my ma, I guess. She hated Dublin—she was a country girl. Said Dublin people were snobs and West-Brits. Said they looked down their noses at country people—called her a culchie. Maybe if I went down to rural Ireland, down to the bog, I'd feel some ancient stirring, something deeper than the bleak and shallow vision my mother passed along to me. She said country people were almost as bad as Dublin people. They were ignorant, often drunk, and they treated women like cattle. She said it rained three hundred and sixty-four out of three hundred and sixty-five. She said she was raised solely to make babies. The only other option was export, eggs for the diaspora. She left when she was seventeen and never went back. She cut the power, tore out the fuse box, left me with no dangling wires I could touch together to jump-start the tradition.

The Apostle John and the City Centre AirBnB

We were in separate apartments, fourth floor of a Victorian tenement, near the city centre—what the Dubliners called the downtown. My window looked out on an iron footbridge that spanned the river. On the other side of that bridge was party central, the pub district, streets and streets of bars. The place, which they even called "Temple," was jammed tight every day—from lunchtime to the small hours, citizens and foreigners shoulder-to-shoulder, pub-crawling through a tide of pizza boxes and fast-food wrappers. Stag parties listed and staggered. Grooms wore diapers or dragged balls and chains. One doomed specimen, in top hat and tails, carried a ten-foot plastic crucifix. His best buddies—Simons all—ran support, picked up the betrothed when he fell, held him when he racked over to vomit. Sometimes the crowd made like the Red Sea to let gangs of sports fans—soccer, rugby, camogie (huh?), hurling (what the fuck?)—through, joining in with their sinister chants. Meanwhile, junkies ghosted the periphery, waiting for an opportunity to snatch and grab. Cop cars parked discreetly down the side streets, seemingly unwilling to get involved unless an all-out melee started up. Taxis lined up along the quays and waited to ferry the near-dead across the river. The place seemed to specialize in stagette parties, groups of loaded women from all over Ireland and England and from as far away as Poland. All of them on the rip—out on the batter, as the locals would say. Benign hens in funny hats, bunny ears, flashing horn-rimmed glasses. Savage hens in every kind of slut outfit getting sluttier as the night went on. Louder, too, and more violent. The seven nights I spent on Bachelor's Quay, my sleep was fucked up every single night—without exception—by the sound of women baiting each other, or confronting the local police. These Irish women were some hard bitches.

"I know ya want to roide me. It's written all over yer bleedin' face."

"That fucking slut came on to me little brother."

"Go back down the country; there's a smell of cow shite off yeh."

The whole place alive and pulsing like a torn gum—the wisdom pulled out with vice grips, the whiskey anaesthetic wearing off. And then, between four and five in the morning, it suddenly stopped. Went battlefield quiet like someone had thrown a blanket over the whole area.

Quiet enough to hear the seagulls. Took me back to my Staten Island home.

But by then I was too awake to sleep. Nothing to do but smoke, lie there, and think about all the Irish writers I had never read. Think about their inspiration. Listen to Floss and Budsy getting their freak on in the next room. Whatever happened on the Camino sure seemed to have renewed that relationship to the extent they were pretending they were on some second honeymoon. All doe-eyes and handholding, sneaking kisses at the dinner table. I was glad when they gave me a list of things to do. I was only too glad not to be around those two.

Budsy and Floss

Budsy needed time to get his head in gear for his performance—a process that involved much sketching on notepads, much drinking of wine, much smoking of spliffs. In between, he paced around the flat in full riot gear—green high tops, orange jumpsuit, black balaclava, chanting old poetry out loud:

> I draw my knowledge from the famous cauldron,
> The breath of nine muses keeps it boiling.
> Is not the head of Annwn's cauldron so shaped:
> Ridged with enamel, rimmed with pearl?
> It will not boil the cowardly traitor's portion.

He stung himself with nettles he picked from abandoned lots around the city centre.

He was Daniel Day-Lewis, getting in character. He was Mr. Bullshit.

His process allowed for plenty of breaks when he'd skip across the bridge to the pub district, or go next door for sushi.

Meanwhile, Floss was spending most of her time at the site, getting everything ready. There were problems, naturally.

The bespoke table on which Budsy was going to set up his centrepiece didn't spin smoothly on its base. It had a hitch in its giddy-up and would only turn about ninety degrees before the ball bearings crunched and the whole thing just ground to a stop.

The carpenter wouldn't touch it because he said the problem was not with the table, but with the base. Some problem with the revolving mechanism.

I told the motherfucker he shoulda been a lawyer—correction—a barrister.

Luckily, the Biggest House in All of Ireland had its own handyman.

It was his idea to replace the 1/8" bearings with 1/4" bearings, which made the table bump where it used to grind, so that the whole thing moved like a slightly warped record. But it worked.

With all the steam and lasers, Floss said no one would notice.

Once the table was sorted out, Floss had to oversee having video screens and speakers installed, gas lines and burners added, and the programs and exhibit cards printed.

The Apostle John's Tasks

I was the runner, the gopher. I was Radar O'Reilly but without the local know-how. I was on a scavenger hunt from hell. My two trickiest tasks were locating a couple of giant witch cauldrons and sourcing a variety of wild game.

Wasn't sure what Budsy planned on doing with that much meat. Maybe he was going to feed the guests. Maybe this was gonna be

some kind of Last Supper deal. I asked. Budsy told me wait and
see. Floss wasn't saying nothing neither.

Secrecy would give the project heat.

It was going to be a surprise.

They spoke as one.

Two was now one.

Wild Game

Floss gave me a list of animals we could use. They mostly had
to be small. No oxen. No giraffe. Nothing bigger than a donkey.
"Fantastic if you can get a monkey," she said, "though not strictly
necessary."

The only non-negotiable was rabbit. We had to have at least
six skinned rabbits and we needed their pelts "on the side." Hares
would do in a pinch. Cats, if there was an absolute shortage of
bunnies. Floss was sure the local SPCA would provide if I gave
them the right incentive.

I googled "wild game," "meats," and "Ireland," and found the
phone number for some farm in Kildare, not far outside Dublin.

"Hello. Waldron's Game."

"Hi, yes, is this Waldron's Wild Meats?"

There was a click and a clunk on the line. A recording of a
man's voice began to play, a deep baritone, his accent mid-Atlantic. "Waldron's Game is operated strictly in accordance with
current European and Irish legislation. Copies of our documen-
tation can be inspected on the premises by prior arrangement.
The principal legislation applicable to the Company is as follows:
European Communities (Food and Feed Hygiene) Regulations
2005. (S.I. No. 910 of 2005) European Communities Regulations
852/2004, 853/2004, 882/2004."

"Hello. Waldron's Game. Hello?"

"Hi. Yes. I can hear you. Can you hear me?"

"The premises are fully approved by the Department of Agriculture and have been granted establishment number IE 2543 EC. They have also been inspected and approved by representatives of the European Community for the export of wild-game products. A government veterinary officer visits the premises on a daily basis for the purposes of monitoring compliance with all relevant legislation and other standards. The veterinary officer also carries out post-mortem examination on carcasses delivered to the premises prior to the commencement of any production activity and during process stages."

"Waldron Meats. Mary speaking. Hello?"

"Hello, Mary. My name is . . ."

"Waldron's Game facilities are run under strict food-safety management systems according to the principles of HACCP (Hazard Analysis & Critical Control Point). A full hazard analysis has been carried out on all stages of food storage, handling, and delivery. All animals are delivered within an acceptable time and placed into refrigerated storage. Large game is stored at -7°C or below and small game at -4°C or below."

"Mary, I can just about hear you . . . the recording. . ."

"Mary speaking. Go ahead please."

"Dressing is carried out in areas operating at or below 12°C and products are returned immediately to refrigerated storage after processing. Critical control steps are in place at every stage to ensure quality assurance of products. All products are packaged and labelled in accordance with current legislation. Labelling is applied to both inner and outer packaging and includes storage requirements and the minimum durability of the product."

There was a loud beep and the recording stopped.

"Hello Mary. My name is John Lopez. I am calling from Dublin."

"Yes, Mr. Lopez. I am so sorry about that. We recently changed IT carriers and the voicemail seems to have a glitch."

"No kidding."

"How can we help you?"

"I am looking for a variety of small game and I need it delivered to an address in Howth by Friday morning at the latest."

"That should not be a problem, sir. What kind of game are you looking for and how much of it? We usually accept advance orders and don't keep that much fresh stock on the premises. Would frozen suit you?"

"That depends on if it is butchered or if it is the whole animal. I need whole animals and I need them skinned. In the case of rabbits, I will need the pelts, too."

"Oh, I see. We have rabbits in just this morning. How many would you need?"

"Six should do it. With the pelts separate. What else do you have?"

"Mostly fowl at the moment: pheasant, mallard, woodpigeon, and snipe. And we are expecting venison tomorrow."

"Terrific. I'll have six of each and one whole deer, skinned but not butchered."

"Do you need the deer pelt?"

"No. But I could use some feathers. If you have feathers from the pheasants and mallards, could you send a couple of bags of those along?"

"You're American. You have a lovely accent."

"Hey, it's youse that has the accent. Not me."

She laughed. "We can have those to you by Friday morning. Actually, we can have them to you by Thursday if you would prefer."

"Beautiful."

"Now if I can have your credit card number and the address?"

The Cauldrons

Easy meat but the cauldrons proved more of a challenge. I knew the kind Floss wanted: the kind witches and their apprentice bitches brewed their potent potions in. The heavy, pot-bellied,

crock-of-gold kind, with a little tam lid that fit snug. The kind
Macbeth's crones would've stirred, squirting beestings into the
broth from their flappy tits. Small, cast-iron versions could be
found at most garden centres. But small would not do. No, sir.
Floss wanted mega-size, fifty-gallon capacity.

I tried antiques shops.

I tried big-box stores.

I was even directed to a blacksmith shop where a serious lep-
rechaun in a leather apron told me my best chance of finding
something like that was down the country, in old barns or sheds.
You even see them in people's front gardens sometimes, he said,
used as planters for red-hot pokers or monkey-puzzle trees.

There were nada cauldrons to be found in Dublin.

Tuesday and Wednesday slipped by.

Every avenue of inquiry turned into a dead end full of wild
geese.

I hit kitchen-supply stores, wholesalers. Probably should have
thought of that first. I hoped Floss would settle for stockpots.
Maybe galvanized bath-pans would do. The kind Budsy said he
got plopped into every Saturday night as a kid. Said he used play
toy cowboys and Indians in one of those tubs. His favourite trick
was to unseat the bow-legged chief from his piebald mount and
reseat him on his prick. "First boner I remember," he said.

One place had stockpots big enough, but the owner—some
officious, weasel-faced ginger with a lisp—wouldn't sell them to
me because I wasn't a licensed restaurant owner. He wouldn't say
why this was important, which could mean only one thing: he
was a racist.

Finally, I found a place that agreed to rent me two sixty-five
gallon stainless-steel stockpots. I signed the agreement, promised
to have them back by Saturday afternoon—they were needed for
some other event that night—knowing full well I wouldn't get
them back in time. In fact, I wasn't going to return them at all.
MiCS and his staff could deal with the fallout.

Because Sunday at noon I was flying back to the States.

The Set-up

It was almost lunchtime on Thursday when I cruised up to the MiCS mansion. On the way there, my taxi driver, a Ghanaian, took pains to explain his theory about why black Americans weren't really black anymore. "If they want to be black men again they must move back to Africa. They must bring lots of investment with them. They must enrich their homelands. In return, Africa will enrich them."

"What if they Africans from the Dominican Republic? Where they supposed to bring the money then?" I asked him. No answer.

Once I wrestled the pots from the back seat (no help from the armchair sociologist), I threw the fare and an extra-generous tip on the front seat. I just wanted to see this bushbaby's buck-tooth grin. "The blessing of Jesus on you," he said, making a sign of the cross in the air. I should've known he was a Bible-thumper. True arrogance cemented by true faith makes for one ignant mo'fucka.

I wasn't in the mood for Floss, who was in a mood. She met me at the front door, drawn outside by the cymbal crash of pot lids on the brick walkway.

"Stainless-steel stockpots? Really? These are going to ruin the aesthetic. I can't believe cauldrons can't be found. Try calling talk radio."

I didn't answer.

"Not a problem," said Budsy, who was already drunk. Hard to say whether the previous night's load hadn't worn off yet or if he'd started early today. But you could smell him from across the room.

"We just need to change the background music to something industrial. The voiceover can be distorted to make it sound like Rob Zombie. Might actually work better."

"Also, there's a problem with the game," Floss said. "Guy delivered it an hour ago. It's in the cold room off the kitchen."

"What's the problem?"

"The rabbits. The fucking rabbits. You're going to have to deal with it."

I ditched Budsy and Floss in the foyer, walked through the kitchen, and opened the frosted door to the chilled pantry. A mountain of meat was stacked on the counters. On one side, a deer carcass, still bleeding. On the other side, fowl bundled together by species and stacked into pyramids. Next to them, hanging on a hook, six brown rabbits, all with their fine, lustrous pelts attached. Mary must have misunderstood.

The Fucking Rabbits

Back in the kitchen, I rooted around until I found a drawer full of sharp knives. Marcel—maybe drawn by the racket I was making—entered with a flourish.

"A laptop, Marcel! My kingdom for a laptop!"

"iPad OK?"

"Yes."

"In the living room next to the couch."

Ten minutes later, I was in one of the guest bathrooms, six rabbits stacked in the bottom of the tub, blade on the counter by the sink. Next to me was the iPad on which I'd cued up a number of videos about how to "dress" rabbits, by which they meant undress the rabbits and butcher them. Easy-peasy.

I picked up the first brown specimen. Snicking the fur on its back thighs, I reached a finger inside and pulled. The pelt came away easily, revealing the purple-pink flesh underneath.

I did the same thing to the second thigh. I was able to pull the skin off the back legs completely, leaving the little guy with his pants down but still wearing his furry boots.

I then made a cut in the pelt just over the bob tail until I could get my fingers underneath. The flesh was slippery and wet, like the inside of a cheek. Room temperature, not cold. Poor bunny wasn't long dead.

I pulled downward and the whole pelt rolled away easily, like tights rolling down a leg. Made a sound like Scotch tape slowly being pulled from the roll. Every now and then there was a sound like stitches popping.

The inside of the pelt was yellow-white, with a thick layer of fat along the belly. The membrane between the pelt and the skin was transparent. It had a blueish cast, like a sausage casing.

Things got a bit *Scarface* when I reached the front paws and neck: the scene in the motel room where the Columbian dealers tie the guy up in the shower and trim his limbs with a chainsaw.

In my frustration, I yanked too hard and managed to rip off the head and one front leg.

I watched the video again and saw my mistake. You were supposed to cut off the head before the skinning.

The process went smoother the second time. By my third bunny, I was an expert. By the fourth and fifth, I was timing myself to see how fast I could go. I was the Carl Lewis of rabbit skinners.

Half an hour later, I returned the dressed rabbits to the pantry, their carcasses naked except for the fur on their back feet and the scut tails, which made them look like stripper-rabbits from back in the day when Commissioner Lapin still insisted on a modicum of decorum.

I went back to the bathroom and gathered up the pelts in a white towel.

The bathtub was full-on De Palma: blood, flesh, and pieces of fur everywhere: lining the bottom of the tub, splattered on the white tiles; globules of fat clinging to the shower curtain. Maybe no one would notice until some poor guest (oxymoron around here) wandered away on the evening of the big event and just happened to pop into this out-of-the-way bathroom for a quick piss. Maybe they'd scream. What would they tell the other guests?

I ran into Floss in the hallway and handed over the bundled pelts.

"The rabbit pelts," I said, trying not to look overly self-satisfied at my own handiwork. "The rabbits and the rest of the game are ready now in the pantry."

She handed the pelts right back. "Do you think you could find me some hair dye and bleach these blonde? Also. I need some black plums, and about a dozen hard-boiled eggs."

"What the fuck?"

"I know. I know. It's asking a lot."

The Apostle John on the Mezzanine

Thirty-six hours later, I stood on the mezzanine looking down on the foyer at poor Marcel. MiCS (maybe as a gift to his sister) insisted that Marcel and all the other workers—ushers, valets, and anyone serving drinks or trays of nibblies—get rigged out as harlequins. Marcel was making the best of it. He wore classic black and red, with an outrageously padded crotch. A fool's cap with gold bells. His face painted like a panda. Shoes with big silver buckles. If MiCS intended to humiliate him so he'd relinquish any claim to his sister's fortune, it wasn't working. Marcel thrust himself around the place, balls first. Did a pirouette in the foyer. Clapped his hands three times. "Ten minutes, mesdames et monsieurs," he announced. He then whipped out the two barbecue lighters he'd holstered on each hip and lit the burners under the great stainless-steel pots positioned on either side of the enormous, custom-made revolving table, which was covered in a cream linen cloth.

"Ten minutes," he said again, "or whenever the broth begins to bubble."

The mezzanine level was packed, mostly with business types—dealers, gallery owners, buyers, curators. Dabbled among them were some artists—you could identify them by their silence, their black clothes, anxieties reefing under bored-bordering-on-disdainful expressions.

The crowd was well-lubricated—folks downing their third or fourth cocktails; the warm spirits animating the medicated wilderness of their collective inner lives. It was the age, after all, in which pharmaceutical companies had invaded the mortar of the soul and successfully pestled to fine powder the uncreated conscience of the human race.

Social fears becalmed, the rich folk pontificated with the confidence unique to their class, their language a raw cocktail of greed and pride. A dealer or businessman behind me regaled a group, speculating wildly on a major Mondrian that had just popped up on the market as part of an estate sale. He was showing them a picture of it on his hand-held device: "I can't help it, but whenever I look at this I think of a floor plan. Something high up—front corner on Park, say. The outside rectangles—if you look carefully—are bitten ever so slightly at the exterior edge by a fine green, almost a primavera. But there are sootier spots as well, and also some border areas have a bright gleam, almost like the sun reflecting off a polished rail. When you look here, at this tiny grey square, it looks like he shaded it to give it depth. Look at that. Do you see it? Look at it long enough and you fall, like down an elevator shaft. Now move inside to the interior and the colours are so complementary that the whole space—while still highly individualized—has an open-plan feel to it. You get that sense of height and light. The light activates your mind's eye. Fantasy vistas appear at the peripheries; at least they do for me, every fucking time.

"It's wild.

"And see here? This deep-yellow square says gathering, party, entertainment. It's being encroached upon by this small, red-orange rectangle. A fireplace? Yes. Big enough to be woodburning. Once you see it you can't not see it. Behind it, this tiny charcoal square just has to be the chimney. So cunning. The formal dining room also faces north. What else could that long, blonde wood shape be but an elegant table? Yes. I suppose it could be a coffin.

"And here we find the soft blue-whites of the bedroom. And in the ensuite, harsher whites, slightly textured with waves to signify water. And note how he made the outlines in these squares heavier, signifying privacy.

"Mondrian painted this in 1929, and it's been hanging in one of the classic New York apartment houses until just last year. It's never been shown publicly. You can look at this painting every day, year in year out, and find something new in it each time. Which explains why the owner never tired of it. The secret? It is not overdetermined, overproduced.

"Now here's the super-interesting thing, the financing. The dealer has set it up like a mortgage. The asking price is five million at 4 percent interest. He will accept a downpayment of 20 percent. That means your monthly payment is $12,000 over forty years. It's an investment, right? In 2050 that investment is going to return way more than five million. The beauty of it is that it puts high-end, museum-quality pieces within the reach of relatively modest earners. It's the future, baby."

Floss was at the other end of the mezzanine, working the crowd. She was excited. I could tell by her exaggerated gestures, by the way she kept grooming her hair. From time to time her voice took on a brassy edge, blared above the male drawl and sibilant female chatter, turning every head except for those hard-of-hearing.

MiCS had not lied. Motherfucker was straight up this time. As far as I could tell, it was a who's who of the European art world. A bling fest. I was surprised to feel excited. Fizzed for Floss—this was the Grammys for her. I had never seen her so tense and so fierce at the same time. She was practically bouncing—a Beyoncé ball. Bubbling for Budsy, who no doubt was downstairs in the kitchen dying a thousand deaths, as he always did, frantically monitoring his inner environment, which at that moment would be a precarious balance of intoxicants.

I made up my mind not to see him until after it was over.

This was it for me.

My swansong.

My last night in the art world.

Budsy would have to get used to operating on his own.

Floss had slowly taken over my role as aide, confidante, supporter, midnight runner, vomit-swabber, and butt-wiper. My work babysitting the world's biggest baby was done now. She could wash his onesies for him.

So I was feeling nostalgic as I waited for the show to start—a brother would have to be soul-dead not to be just a little. But I was also feeling the first stirrings of a new life that I was not even close to properly conceiving. Tomorrow. I was flying back to New York, where I'd pack up before heading to California.

Land of the grape.

Land of the sun and the string bikini.

I had a yen to explore the Baha Peninsula, a destination I had picked by throwing a dart on a map, a place name I had read by sound, and so misread. Baja black sheep.

He Moved Through the Fair

I zigzagged my way through the crowd of elegantly robed and fragrance-enhanced white bodies. The gathering had reached the critical mass at which individuals merged into the collective. The stratum had accreted the herd number, the quantity of buffalo it took not to be intimidated by the lion in their midst, that is, by a brother among them who was not serving drinks.

I wanted to stand next to Floss when the show started. I needed her Piranha presence.

Skeins of conversation wound around me like bindweed, truths, half-truths, and obvious lies blaring into both ears through silk trumpet flowers.

"This is Saffron: 'Joss' Mudd's nephew."

Someone nearby was TALKING about the cost of injecting value into someone's catalogue raisonné. I thought of Tito, my

pastry-chef friend, standing in the back room of his Bronx patis-
serie, injecting fresh cream into chocolate eclairs. I missed him.

"You can't be serious. Crazy old bat. Her heyday was between
the wars."

"A one-time model for Léger."

"You don't say."

Who? I wanted to know. Wanted to butt in. But raised eyebrows were chevrons warning me away. A salvo of deconstructiv-
ist, modernist, and kineticist pins flew past like hornets. How I
wished at that moment I was bearing a tray of canapés.

"A painter and a sculptor. A contemporary of Georges Bunga-
low, Jean Horan, and Minnie Beak."

Not Minnie Beak of Finchley, daughter of the grossly rich
operatic tenor? Then did a check-in on myself for being this way.
So clever. So reflex-ready to use irony to shut down, twist-shut
the cap on my better self.

"She abused—one critic went so far as to say *raped*—the narratives that could include her. Her resistance to categorization—
her willingness to stick it to the man—is unignorably a factor in
her obscurity; she was left out because she refused to fit in."

Was that a loose tautology? And why did the thought that I
could have such a thought feel like my own dark eulogy? I had
entered the field of contagion. When had I contracted counterfeit? Why could I not admit to the buboes in my armpit, in my
groin fork. It was end-of-days stuff. I was close to panic. Once
again I tuned in to Floss's laughter, caught a glimpse of her Bot-
ticelli ringlets.

I parted the body sea with an outstretched hand and open
palm, I swivelled, hipped, and shimmied through. Thank you
very much. Thank you.

"The work is impressive, generously proportioned with lake
and ocean views, with sand and surf motifs. The four panels allow
plenty of room for study, dreaming, and storage. The colours are
luxurious. The brushwork sleek and stylish. The main panel has

the texture of furs and brocade. The side panels have all the privacy and austerity of a dentist's office."

I cannonballed away. But wait, what's this? A flutter-by buttering in Ecuador shifted my testicular pendulum away from stasis, making my sad heart skip a beat. Before me: two hot chicks in micro-minis, art students or artists or both. Bona-fide babes with enough booty to make the illiterate alliterate.

"So there was this white rope hanging from the ceiling. So soft-looking. The rope not the ceiling. OMG What are you—on acid? OMG Anyway. I was like so drawn to it but I couldn't say why? Ya, so. It was less an *a-ha* moment than it was an *oh-o* moment. Or maybe it was the other way around. I was positively and negatively persuaded and assaulted by the possibilities and interpretations of the piece. Yeah. I totally got that bit from my professor. No, I'm not sleeping with him, bitch."

I could not pass these girls. Had to try my luck. Nothing was over. I knew this the second my Converse sole hit the brake. Ma, I had still to procreate. I had no choice but to share my inner puppy with them. We would have coffee, tea, a walk by the cold Irish ocean. Hold hands on the first date. Not suck face until the fourth. Love at first sight! Before committing, we would send our spit tubes to the Mormon Underground Chapel. Ignore the commodity of the body until sanctioned by genetic, episcopal, and legal green lights. I had it bad. The happy apple in my head sounded church bells.

"A stupid reading would have been to see that dangling rope as a way up, some metaphorical climb out of nothingness into something. Ya. But there was a gravity about it. It got up my nose. Like right into the nasal cavity. The piece felt to me more about coming down. That sense of being stuck in the gore. Bloodied even. Brought down to the level of the earth. The body. It was all in the white softness of that rope, and the gently twirled knot at its end."

In response to my stopping by their woods, my pearly whites on high beam, they both sent *Mr. Freezie* looks of terror my way.

A giant figurative policeman loomed over my shoulder, night stick inappropriately poking, and told me to move on.

There, near Floss, a well-known British dealer—renowned for his bow ties and love of poppers—yacked at a couple of gallery owners.

Nearer still was that big Irish actor with the broken nose; he was dredging vowels and sifting consonants, reciting some lines: "Just then the sunshine reappeared and set ablaze the holding pens ahead. There came the sound of flies, their agitating wings, like Latin whispers from a congregation. Before us a pen filled with black-face sheep, their tongues stuck out, as children for a wafer of communion. The butcher standing at the hoof-scarred door, his shirt sleeves rolled, his forehead slick with sweat. He was dressed in rubber from head to toe, fresh from the field, the dragon slain, the carcass skinned and steaming on the floor, the deadbolt gun behind it on a hook."

I gave him a bro nod, passing right along.

I was in deep-scan mode. Like my brain had downloaded some facial-recognition app and I was using it to troll. I could thank Floss's Facebook and Google-image tutorials for this. She trained me to identify faces and match them with credentials. Here a Venice Biennale, here a MoMA, there a Tate Modern. Old MiCS-Donald had a farm. An artist who had exhibited at one of these three automatically got four stars. The screen turned pink and the quartet flashed if the artist had exhibited at two of the three institutions. Having had work in all three made the phone throb in my hand, made the camera eye weep a silicone tear.

Salesforce Floss

By the time I reached Floss, I was ready to heave my guts upon the travertine marble tiles. I was so not going to miss all this. I had rotten molars I'd mourn more than the biz. Didn't matter if you were in a storefront gallery in Boise or on the floor of the Museum of Modern Art; it was the same the river of horseshit pretending to be—I don't even know what—a cup of crystal-clear mountain truth maybe.

Effluent in dreamland.

This shit was heroin in need of an opioid antagonist.

Floss was talking to a group of older women, all of them tanned, moisturized, and bejewelled. She was telling them about the Camino, about the legend of the Hanged Innocent, something she'd read to me from a guidebook when we were over there.

"So this pilgrim doing the Camino is falsely accused of theft. This was back in Renaissance times. The judge sentences him to hang. Later, the judge is stopped by a sage outside the courthouse and told that when he sits down to eat his roast-chicken dinner that night, a cock will crow. A sage. Not the herb. You know, a seer, some kind of local holy man; so the cock crowing would be a sign to the judge that the sentenced pilgrim is innocent."

"Reminds me of my wedding night."

"I don't get it. Wait, I get it."

"What? Maybe he ate roast chicken every night. I don't know."

"My dears, let her tell her story."

"Thank you, Elsie. The point is this: the cock did crow that night, just as the judge was about to have his dinner. And the pilgrim was saved."

"Big surprise."

"Let her finish."

"So this event is remembered today at the Santa Domingo de la Clazada cathedral where a pair of live white chickens—a hen and a rooster—are kept in a glass henhouse. Pilgrims can buy souvenir feathers from these birds."

"I'd be afraid of lice."

"You can also buy *milagros del santo*, or "miracle of the saint" chicken-shaped pastries in the local bakeries."

"I've had those. In Galway, Eyre Square, of all places.

"Some people think it's cruel to the chickens. . . No, not to make them into pastries—to display them in a glass box. You would have fit right in with the PETA crowd who were protesting there the day we visited. It was hilarious. A fight broke out between them and the local police."

That was my girl, spinning a tale from the guidebook as though we had really been there. We hadn't made it as far as the Santa Domingo de la Clazada cathedral. Not even close. And the detail about the animal-rights activists—what can I say? Good copy.

I thought about calling her bluff, just to see how badly she might maul me. But just then the lights dimmed in the foyer. People on the mezzanine turned as one to look down.

Green lasers shot down from the ceiling to illuminate the giant stainless-steel pots that were now boiling.

From speakers came the sound of a sheep bleating.

A giant video screen, mounted on a portable gibbet and angled slightly upward—so it could be easily read by the folks looking down—flashed into life.

A title appeared: *Fair Game.*

From speakers came the sound of a bandsaw. Sheep bleating.

The title occupied the screen for about thirty seconds and then slowly began to ascend, drawing in its wake the exhibit statement:

Fair Game

Fair Game manipulates biological structures in order to deconstruct socially defined spaces and how we use them in a context both surreal and analytical.

Fair Game probes the dialectic between what is retained and what is lost, the derelict present that was once entrepreneurial, and the new growth forcing its way in a hothouse of entropy.

Fair Game cross-examines, inquires, scrambles, transmutes, destabilizes, collages, dislocates—though often it doesn't do these things so much as it pretends to, pretends not to, or it may actually do what it pretends.

Fair Game's meat sculpture pecks at a void that signifies precisely the corporality of that which it represents.

Fair Game is a suggestive mind game involving the viewer with the making process, complicating instinctive responses to this murder assemblage.

Fair Game centres on an interest in the universality of our biological make-up, on the miracle of making, showing, disregard, and natural decline; combined with the collective sense of the sublime.

Fair Game practices hesitation as part of the process of decision-making, where the object is neither the object of thingness nor the art-object. It is rather the slant object of the artist's conception.

Fair Game explores the relationship between the body and talk radio, between desire and waste, between waist and trouser size; the relationship between the ubiquitous myth and genetic gifts.

In the beginning was the Centre.
And the Centre was with God.

The Show

A burst of nervous laughter erupted from the spectator gallery followed by a smattering of applause. The room went dark except for the tailings-pond-green glow of the laser pods and the fading gray shimmer of the video screen.

From speakers came the sound of a sheep bleating.

From speakers came the sound of a bone saw.

As clapping sputtered out, people slowly became aware of a doorbell ringing—actually a buzzer, not a bell. Folks nearest to the edge of the balcony strained over the railing in an attempt to see. Those on the ground floor either turned to face the door or craned necks to look back over a shoulder.

A recording of a single military drum began to play at low volume.

From speakers came the sound of a sheep bleating.

Two small children (Marcel's?) dressed as flower fairies skipped into view. Each child carried a pillowcase from which they strewed on the floor before them handfuls of brilliantly coloured feathers— the mallard's metallic-green plumage, the pheasant's imbricated russets and blacks. Running out of feathers, they each removed a small primrose posy from the bottom of their pillowcases, which they presented with a curtsey to Floss, who was standing to the left side of the performance area. She kissed the little girls once on each cheek, before pulling them close to her. She brought the small bouquets to her nose, holding them there.

Two lines of harlequins—humans, not ducks—came behind, each person carrying a large metal tray stacked with meat: teepee of pheasant, barrow of snipe, plateau of mallard, stacked cord of rabbit. The mineral smell of raw meat and blood began to infil-trate—it brought to mind a picture I once saw in a library book: a pyramid of severed Vietnamese heads stacked on the lawn of a French colonial home, while, nearby, white people sat at a table drinking tea, eating cake.

The troupe was rounded out by two more harlequins carrying a skinned deer strung by its legs from a birch pole. A few people began to clap for this, but they were drowned out.

From speakers, louder and with greater frequency, came the sound of a bandsaw.

Budsy stepped out of the shadows dressed in his usual uniform: orange jumpsuit, green sneakers, and black ski mask. He flipped the switch on two yellow hand-beacons and, with sweeping circular motions, guided the harlequin pairs to the left and to the right. They rounded to the area immediately behind him, where they crassly dumped the meats onto trestle tables.

On a signal from Budsy, they again formed into two lines, facing one another. A second signal set them to raise the trays above their heads and begin smashing them together. But in a courtly way, like they were some kind of industrial morris dancers. The sound, which at first made me think of a cheesy B-flick storm scene, soon increased to cacophony, steel drums of the damned, hammers smashing on garbage cans or rocks raining down on galvanized rooftops.

On a whistle blast from Budsy, they stopped: the harlequins lowered their trays and quietly filed out through the kitchen doors.

From speakers came the sound of a sheep bleating.

From speakers came the sound of a bone saw.

Budsy walked over to the dudes carrying the deer, made an X in front of his face with his marshalling light wands before pointing them at the floor.

The bearers shrugged off their load, letting the carcass drop. The skinned animal hit the tiles with a resounding, fleshy smack, like some roly-poly falling flat on a swimming-pool deck. My mind played a slide show of skinned hands and knees from my childhood before short-circuiting to a more triple-X Act Two: the last frantic moments of doggy-style fucking, thigh slapping thigh, thigh slapping thigh, rump flesh palpitating.

A woman on the mezzanine grimaced. "I don't know if I can do this," she said loudly to her companion in mink. The fact that we could all hear her made me realize how quiet everyone had become.

From speakers came the sound of a sheep bleating.

Budsy turned off his hand beacons.

He stood in the half dark with his arms folded, his head panning slowly left to right and right to left across the spectator gallery. He had everyone's attention. The lights came up a little, enough that he could see faces all the way to the back of the room. Were he a politician he would, at that moment, have picked out—or pretended to pick out—people he knew. He would have waved—Oh, hi!—to no one in particular. He would have done the point and nod. But Budsy was not interested in breaking the tension. He was not interested in creating intimacy or humanizing the gathering.

Twice he stuck out his tongue and wiggled it around—a shocking dart of pink against his black woollen headgear. I could just about see his eyes, glittering and unblinking, puddles in the balaclava sockets' potholes. He was on some kind of chemical, way stoned. Another sharp chirp from a referee's whistle set him in motion. He walked quickly across the room to where Floss stood in the wings. He began to growl and snarl. The two flower fairies attempted to hide behind Floss.

"Run. You better run; you little fuckers," Budsy roared, aiming a kick that almost connected with one of the little girls as she ran past him screaming. "This is no place for brats."

An audible intake of breath from the audience.

A hidden camera caught his trajectory from behind. He was a man on a mission and he was closing in. At the last second, the video angle changed so it was Floss who appeared on the screen, her look of bemusement turning to surprise when he raised his hand and struck her hard across the face—the sound of impact a breaking stick.

Gasp from the audience, who, to a person, flinched, or was it that they all simultaneously did a double-take? Looked from live action to screen to confirm if what had happened had really happened.

The camera stayed focused on Floss's face, now partially eclipsed by the back of Budsy's head. Her eyes brimmed.

"That's assault," an audience member said, "sexual assault."

Floss smiled as though returning a smile from Budsy. We watched as he leaned in, kissed her cheek in the place where his finger welts had just started to appear. He returned to the centre of the stage. The atmosphere in the room was suddenly partisan, hostile.

From speakers came the sound of a sheep bleating.

From speakers came the sound of a bone saw.

Then a Disembodied Voice (Budsy doing his bad impression of Ezra Pound reciting): "Dead leaves collect along the terraced steps. I look across the windswept college square, towards the student centre where we met. Maple leaves, one or two still marbled green, but most are russet, orange or the brown-red of livers, spleens, beef hearts sliced in two—all colours I have traced out in your hair."

From speakers came the sound of a sheep bleating.

From speakers came the sound of a bone saw.

Budsy feinted left before turning right and casually strode over to one of the meat-laden tables. Grabbing a bird carcass in each hand, he dropped one in one pot and one in the other. He turned up the gas so that the flames tongued the undersides of the vessels and blackened their stainless-steel sides. He dropped more meat in each pot until the water in both spilled over the top and down the sides, bubbling and hissing into the flames, a grey gruel of it oozing across the tabletop and spilling in a needle-thin stream to the floor.

The steamy air started to smell sickeningly of boiling meat. Like a cafeteria in some downtown homeless shelter. With it came the smell of stale sweat in unwashed clothes. The smell of effort souring in body crevices just before it bloomed into sweet and saintly BO. That boiling grey hit every register: yeast crust, fungi sock, green gusset. Remember the skunk-man who sat next to you on the bus, who tested your Christian charity, at least until you brushed past him in disgust? Remember him?

A woman behind me started retching.

The laser light aiming down on the stockpots changed from green to red. More red lasers shot out from the sides of the room—sweeping the space like gunsights.

From speakers came the sound of a sheep bleating. A second sheep bleating. Many sheep, arrhythmic bleats. A blow, hoofs scrabbling and slipping; thump of some heavy thing falling. Sheep chorus: panicked bleating.

Disembodied Voice: "Ramps, double-decked trucks, stink, lights, shouts, kicks, electric prods, coconuts, the workmen's high calypso as beasts run, speed croquet over piss-shellacked and shit-plastered floors, gully and drain-scored."

A harlequin appeared from the kitchen, pushing a stainless-steel trolley on which had been arranged a selection of meat cleavers, butcher's knives, and saws.

"Lock the doors," Budsy commanded. "Nobody leaves this room."

Another harlequin followed, this one pushing an enormous cart piled with white ceramic bowls and stainless-steel spoons. He laid out a dozen place settings on the spotlit trestle table at the back of the stage area. He then removed from a cabinet underneath the cart a stone jug, from which he poured a viscous and stringy red liquid into each white vessel.

"Cold blood. Cold blood. Cold blood," Budsy chanted, before turning and pointing to the entrance: "Lock the doors now."

MiCS stepped out of the shadows and made "calm-the-fuck-down" gestures towards a group nearest the main entrance who suddenly made as if to leave. He mimed reassurance—the doors weren't really going to be locked. This was a show.

From speakers came the sound of a bone saw.

Disembodied Voice: "Inside, no messing in mess. The point driven home, mallet or stun gun sets each one staggering, a modern dance to the skull's high pitch..."

Budsy fell to his knees and started doing something to the deer carcass. Then he hunchbacked in a half crouch to the corner and pulled a chain that hung overhead, and which we could now see ran across the ceiling. The carcass lifted from the floor, rising until it hung in the centre of the room, crisscrossed with red laser beams.

Disembodied Voice: "Orchestral machinery kicks in. The conveyor belt's dangling clefs, a score into which their hooves are hooked. Hoisted, they perform one-leg inverted ballet that turns to opera that turns again into modern dance (the classical forms will not contain) as they flex, wriggle, twist, gyrate all the way to the conductor, whose shiny baton slashes."

Budsy picked up a meat cleaver and a knife and attacked. Carefully at first, as though the laser lines were a butcher's chart of choice cuts that he was trying to follow. Slice by numbers. Soon, however, he was vocalizing like some Japanese warrior and hacking at the meat left and right, cleaver and knife, like this was the enemy who had slaughtered his family, raped his wife and daughters, and boiled his only son alive in a font of holy water.

Disembodied voice: "Out back, crisscrossed with hawsers, some great animal lay dying, its sore-covered hide weeping rivers of pus. The boss would tell us how to speed the flow, how to mask its stink and—nudge-nudge-wink-wink—why the animal, racked in pain and in terror, made no sound when its scabs were hacked off, the wounds drained to fill some last-minute order."

Audience members muttered to each other. Everywhere, expressions of disgust. A few laughed.

Chunks of deer fell to the floor, exposing lightning strikes of bone.

Budsy sawed off the animal's head and kicked it across the floor.

He hacked off its front legs.

He carefully inserted the knife just above the groin and unzipped the abdomen downward, towards the dripping neck. He dropped his tools and reached inside what remained of the deer's carcass, pulling out the contents of its belly, like it was laundry day and he was emptying a dryer full of inflated pantyhose.

Red-blue-purple-pink viscera in coils, vines and lumps slith-
ered and plopped to the floor. He stomped on a dark, bloated area
of intestine. A clot of feces spurted out. He circled the excrement
before doing what looked like a slow soft-shoe number through
it. He turned the shit into ink, using it to smear an Asiatic glyph.

"It means atrocity," someone called down from the balcony.

"No, it's Pepsi in Mandarin."

Budsy walked back to the carcass. He fed out a length of gut
through his fingers until it was long enough to swing. He walked
toward the front row of the audience, scanning the ranks as if
looking for one head he wanted to bullwhip. There was no sound
except for his footsteps, the bubbling pots and the bullroarer
thrum the intestines rope made as he swung it helicopter style.
People ducked, shielded with hands. Some in the rows further
back began to flinch and complain they were getting spattered,
that bits were hitting them. Women began to tuck themselves
against their partners, raise arms to protect their faces.

"Enough already!" Someone shouted.

Budsy stopped. Dropped the coil, ran back to the carcass,
cleaved a hoof from a dismembered foreleg that he then attached
by meathook to the other end of the intestine rope before launching it high toward the mezzanine, where it caught like a grappling
hook in the rail.

Someone screamed. Someone shouted Bravo!

MiCS stepped forward, his face showing concern, but he was
stopped in his tracks by a sprinting Marcel, who gently compelled
the older man to return to his place. All part of the act: like James
Brown helped off stage by his sidekicks.

Budsy yanked the gut rope and it gave way, leaving the fore-
foot entangled in the rail. The intestines came streaming down,
hitting the floor with a slap and sending a spray of what could
only have been blood and liquid shit across the shoes and the
lower legs of those standing closest.

"Ah come on, man."

"Fuck sakes."

"Disgusting."

"Boo! Boo!"

MiCS stepped forward again. Budsy ran away from him, ran back to the carcass and bent over in a way that made me think he was going to try to wedge his butt into the deer's abdominal cavity, turn the whole carcass into a suspended egg chair. He rolled up the balaclava and made hunted faces at those cursing him from the mezzanine.

MiCS made wiper motions with both hands. Marcel once again appeared from the shadows to run interference, this time forcefully pushing MiCS backward until the big man was once more sidelined. The crowd settled back into uneasiness.

Budsy walked forward, picking up the intestine coil and, with all the casual intensity of an experienced yachtsman fashioning a knot, tied a noose at one end, before tying the other end around his waist.

He approached Floss and, with a hesitant bow, placed the noose around her neck. He then walked back towards the carcass, gently towing her behind.

What followed was an even more frenzied attack on the deer. He worked long knife and chopper, carving meat, splintering bones and gristle, his blade work reaching a crazed intensity. He grunted. Bits flew. Liquids dribbled. He stopped to lick blood off his forearms, rolling his eyes in an obscenely suggestive way, as if he were a gargoyle squatting on a sleeping virgin to lap up her menstrual blood.

Watching his sustained assault, my torso started flexing in time with each rhythmic flurry, each hack and stab, each downward slash of the cleaver. Motherfucker was possessed. When he was finished, all that remained was a single hind leg hanging from the ceiling.

The lights came on. He raised his arms to the gallery.

"Processing complete," he announced. "Act II, the Reconstruction."

"Enough! Enough of this!" A man shouted from the mezzanine.

"Let him finish."

"Let the artist do his work."

"He's telling us we can't turn away."

Disembodied Voice (NOW MUCH LOUDER): "Then one holiday, when the shop was thick with customers vying for the last cake or torte, I heard from every aisle a rumble—mackerel thrashing ice to smithereens down at seafood; dull thumps and pops where parsnips and carrots launched salvo after salvo towards asbestos-covered rafters, while over in meats, choreographed by a butcher's chart, shank joined brisket and chum with rump, chop slotted chop with an audible slap, as meat reassembled back into animal."

A projection beamed down from the ceiling, mapping onto the white linen tablecloth the outline of a human face, all portioned up like some paint-by-numbers.

Budsy spun the table hard enough to make it go round several times, the ball-bearing base crackling like some fucked-up roulette wheel. He pulled on a pair of black rubber gloves and walked over to one of the pots. From the grey soup he plucked out handfuls of slimy, half-cooked meat and started placing them carefully into the regions of the face map.

Disembodied Voice: "I watched it list, stagger towards the light, take up position by the sliding doors, where it reached out a red-stamped, stitched, and reconstructed hand to everyone in sight, to those coming in and to those sickened by life, who wished to escape it. Thanks a million, it said, for the farmland and the forage, for the warm barn in winter, for allowing us to thrive while others failed."

The same audience that had been traumatized by savagery moments before now stood transfixed, intrigued by the image emerging on that tablecloth. They pressed forward towards the mezzanine rail. I worried about a collapse.

"Go Budsy."

"*Magnifique.*"

"Mayo for the All-Ireland this year," a man shouted.

There was a burst of laughter.

"Jale. Jale! *Asi se toca!*"

People on the main floor pushed in closer, including MiCS, who was now standing immediately to the right of the table. We folks up in the gallery had the best view. The face would reveal itself to us a lot sooner than it would to those standing closer to it.

A recording of a woman's voice started to play at a low volume. At first it sounded like deep pleasure, a fuck soundtrack, as if she were on the verge of orgasm, about to lose her shit.

People threw each other uncomfortable glances or looked away. A few made sheep's eyes. The sound at once built on the carnage of the previous act, on the rising smell of boiled meat, shit, blood, and viscera, working to create an erotic charge. Somehow it recreated the space that most people only encounter in the bedroom, the kind of experience gifted to the pharmaceutically fucked-up; the moment when inhibitions disappear and all that remains are our deepest, most shameful desires, brazenly revealed to the old God who devours in us everything we thought decent and unselfish.

"Go-wan!"

"Fucking patriarchy."

"Shhhhhhhhsh!"

"Go-wan, Budsy!"

The face slowly filled in. The video screen began to flicker. A blurred image of a woman's torso appeared—was it naked or was that some kind of translucent tie-dyed cloth or body paint?

Now Budsy went to work on the eyes. Black plums for pupils, sliced kiwi for irises, sliced boiled egg whites for the corneas. Yellow egg yolk in the corners—an infection? Through a fine nozzle he squirted the boiled whites with ketchup to make a filigree of burst capillaries. Two tapered snipe wings—still feathered—made eyebrows.

I knew those eyebrows. I knew that expression.

He assembled the mouth from pieces of raw rabbit flesh, inserting blank scrabble tiles for teeth.

The image of the woman's torso flickered on the screen again, and this time held. It wasn't cloth or body paint; she was a map of bruises—black turning yellow-green, a diagonal band running from her left breast down across her ribs.

A murmur ran through the crowd. One woman in the front row began to cry, transforming the man beside her into a cartoon: like he was trying to OJ Simpson his rage into an empathy face that was far too small a fit.

Now Budsy was splotching mustard into the nostrils (two mallard neck cavities) and padding out the right cheek and the upper-right eye with cutlets. He then took a handful of the deer viscera. With gardening shears, he cut it into flaps he arranged until the left side of the face and the right eye looked swollen and bruised.

Hurriedly, he pulled two garbage bags out from under the table. From inside, he snagged the rabbit skins I had bleached and dyed blonde the night before (my hands were still burning). The pelts were quickly arranged in the side-parted hairstyle some of us were so familiar with.

Finally, in what came across almost like an afterthought, but was really the pièce de resistance, he removed two of the scrabble tiles from her mouth, one upper and one lower. The effect was both startling and grotesquely comic, like when you take a marker and black out several teeth on the supermodel gracing the cover of *Vogue*.

The lights dimmed, all except the ones illuminating the table and the place where Budsy stood. He clapped his hands.

"Act III: Retribution."

No one moved. The images of the woman's torso began to flicker on the screen before fixing in place once more. The soundtrack was turned way up. We heard a man—unmistakably MiCS—shouting, his voice high and breathless: "You mangy fucking bridge-and-tunnel *cunt!* You harridan! How dare you try to tell me how to run my business! You *cunt!* I owe you absolutely nothing. *Cunt!*"

"MiCS? Jesus." Floss's voice: "What the fuck? Goddam it, get a GRIP."

MiCS took a step backwards were he stood in the wings but managed only to step into one of the many spotlights now illuminating faces in the crowd. His expression was that of a man fully in the moment, someone grimly weighing his options. He was not yet panicking. A man of MiCS's experience knew that the end was never the end, just another set of possibilities to consider. He had taken that Tony Robbins seminar. MiCS gave the impression that he was listening carefully to the recording, like he was judging his performance. Had to hand it to him; he was one cool hand.

We heard a dull thump, followed by a sharp intake of breath, then another, louder thump.

"Tranny fucking bitch. Always wondered what happened when you punched a silicon tit. Does it burst? Like a tube of glue. Is that it?"

There was a rustling sound like wind blowing into a microphone.

"Get your fucking hands out of the way. Want me to break your fingers? Is that what you want? *Cunt*? Fucking freak *cunt*. Show me them tits."

It was the recording Floss played for us the night we camped on the Meseta—the answering-machine tape from the old flat, the call from the phone that was knocked out of her hand when he beat her.

"You bitch! You think I owe you something? I owe you nothing. I can make you or break you. I don't need you. Freak. I'll show you. Here's how much I fucking need you!"

What followed was the sound of blows falling. Glass breaking. Floss crying out.

"NO, STOP WILL YOU?"

Her words punctuated by gasps, wails, breathlessness.

"YOU'RE HURTING ME. YOU'RE HURTING ME."

Her words punctuated by strikes, fleshy slaps.

"WHY ARE YOU DOING . . .WHAT THE . . .Will you stop?
Her voice getting smaller.
Her words getting fewer.
But never the word *please*.
From speakers came the sound of a bone saw.
Soon there were no words from Floss, just cries and moans, but even those were getting more muted.
Plenty of words from MiCS though. The same bitch-stream of invective, his voice getting more and more strangled. His words falling in rhythm with the blows.
People in the audience hid their faces. Some stared, wide-eyed. Others were clearly shouting words that could not be heard above MiCS ranting.
Cunt! You even have one? Still have balls down there? We'll see about that. You liked that. Want another one? *Cunt!* I'll make a hole for you. One that will never close over. Save you all that money. You will do what I say or you will get this. More of THIS."
MiCS breathing heavily, his words half-aspirated.
"HEAR ME YOU TRANNY *CUNT.*"
There was a hollow sound like someone banging on a door or a wall.
"HEAR ME. YOU EVER WANT TO WORK AGAIN. . ."
I looked down from the balcony on the brutal image of Floss's face created in the style of an Arcimboldo painting. I looked at the bruised torso showing on the video screen. I felt blown open, exposed to something sacred and secret about life: like this rite was iconic, a black-mass veneration, the diseased soul in monstrance.
All the air had gone out of the room.
The lights dimmed.
Now a powerful, handheld spotlight lit up in the shadows and flickered briefly around the corners before coming to rest at the place where MiCS had been standing. The spotlight flicked around, searching.
"He's over there," a woman shouted from the mezzanine. "Sitting down."

MiCS was leaning forward in a chair, elbow resting in hand, chin resting on closed fist. His expression was one of horror. He brought his hand to his face in an effort to hide, a gesture he quickly transformed into something more casual, like he was stroking an imaginary beard.

The image on the screen changed again, this time to what looked like surveillance video from a security camera on the driveway outside the house, a view familiar to everyone attending the performance. Two Irish police cars could be seen making their way up the long drive, blue tops twirling. The soundtrack of Floss's screams stopped and was replaced by the sound of sirens slowly gathering in volume.

All eyes were on MiCS. Three harlequins marched from the performance area and surrounded him; whether to guard him or block his exit, it was hard to say.

Ten, twenty, maybe thirty seconds passed. His expression was fixed, but his eyes betrayed furious thinking, the rat of self-interest frantically exploring his labyrinthine cerebrum.

Finally, when it felt like the room was about to come apart at the seams, he stood up, a smile slowly taking hold of his face. He nodded knowingly to Budsy and, raising his hands, started a slow clap.

For those traumatized by the event, this applause struck us like a series of hard slaps to the face, triggering further pain. Everyone stared straight ahead as if they were afraid to turn and look at whoever was standing next to them, afraid of what they might see or what might be seen on their own faces.

MiCS began to clap harder. He walked in a measured way towards centre stage, his eyes drilling into Budsy's balaclava-covered face. A few in the audience followed his lead. Hesitantly at first. But soon the applause was enough that the atmosphere discharged some of its tension into relief. Of course, it was what they had suspected all along. It was theatre, an experiential happening, an event. And MiCS was just another one of the actors. He'd been in on it all along. People began to say as much aloud. Amazing.

What did it say about him that he would go along with this? So courageous. So cutting edge. The tone was suddenly reassuring. No police officers came charging through the doors. Wasn't this proof? Surely it was. The whole police-car thing had been prerecorded. Of course. Of course. The applause grew. How raw and brave. How audacious.

But it was only when the lights came up and Floss was seen to ceremoniously remove the offal noose from around her neck that the majority were convinced. She skipped over to where Budsy stood, centre stage, and threw her arms around him. After a few moments' embrace, the two of them beckoned wildly toward me, insisting that I join them.

I was making way down the stairs from the mezzanine when I saw MiCS move towards Floss, his arms outstretched as though to embrace her. She shrunk at his approach like plastic before a flame. Again, Marcel flew in from the wings and chest-bumped MiCS several times, backing him away from Floss. How Marcel hated his brother-in-law, and how much he was enjoying the moment was written in the big grin that wouldn't leave his face. MiCS had no choice but to play along, pretend this was a bro-on-bro celebration.

If any of the audience members noticed the continuing interference, they were soon distracted by a small group of the offended making an angry exit. Bloggers and hack columnists. Halfway across the ground floor I did a Brian Boitano, slipped and skidded on my back through a tide of pot-water froth, blood, and viscera. I could feel it soaking through my t-shirt, wetting the back of my head. People laughed. They seemed to think it was all part of the act. I was the black jester.

I took my place, Budsy to my right, Floss next to him; Marcel to my left and MiCS to his left, the farthest distance away from Floss he could be while still joining in the collective bow. We grabbed each other's wrists, the five of us bending forward in unison; then we all raised our arms together, lifting our eyes to the mezzanine level. The applause increased. People cheered and stamped their feet until the whole balcony trembled and I was afraid that, in some final unintended irony, the applause would literally bring the house down.

The Last Word

You think you know what happened. Maybe you do and maybe you don't. People always think they know, even when they weren't there. And even if they were there—you know how often eyewitness testimony puts black man X on death row, only for it to turn out, years later, that X was nowhere near the scene when the crime went down? Eyewitnesses say X pulled the trigger, killed that brother, when in actual fact X was across town barbecuing burgers for his teenage kids. Shee-it. There's always more to art than meets the eye.

I was best friends with Floss and Budsy for years, and even I'm not sure I know exactly what happened that night. What first looked like a simple revenge plot turned out to look more like a business move. Something secretive and common as snot. Ya, I'm talking blackmail.

Floss was deeper than the Mariana Trench.

And Budsy was nowhere near as commercially stupid as he pretended to be. He's the kind of guy stops on a dime, gets himself rear-ended and walks away in a fake neck brace with a wad of insurance cash.

How else to explain what happened in the years following? Floss with galleries in London and Berlin; Budsy with shows at Whitechapel and the Tate; and lately, Budsy on the cover of *Artforum. Artforum!*

I saw the three of them for a short while right after the show. I was all lathered up like a third-run pony in the Kentucky Derby. I was basically foaming at the bit to get the fuck out of there. I was exhilarated, but I was also afraid. Perhaps there was someone

who'd seen through the whole thing, who was now making her
way through the crowd, a fillet knife in her hand, her intention to
sink that thin, steel blade deep into MiCS's mouldy heart.

Up close, neither Floss nor Budsy looked especially trium-
phant. No one had a rosette pinned on their lapel. No one held up
a silver trophy.

Budsy looked shattered, the performance high draining from
him like vital fluids. He always told me being up on stage was an act
of violent exposure. Ain't it weird how introverted motherfuckers
like to show off? Budsy said performing felt like crawling through
a very tight space before expanding to several times your normal
size, as if you were a sponge, only sentient. Performance was mind-
blowing to Budsy—a series of Weegee flashbulbs going off in his
face until the world turned monochrome. Afterwards, he said
he felt naked and exposed. Said the process had to reverse itself in
some cruel way because he had to get smaller. And when he did,
all his adrenalin went sour, turned into major anxiety. Best to get
drunk or high and pass out, he said. Like he needed an excuse.

He was still in the early stages of decompression when I pulled
him aside. He wasn't making a whole lot of sense. He kept hug-
ging me, hot-mouthing in my ear that everything was gonna be
OK; telling me not to go back to New York just yet.

"I gotta go," I said. "Who's gonna feed the fish?"

I hugged Floss. Her body was hard, like she'd been pumping
iron and drinking steroid cocktails all week. She was trembling,
though not in a nervous way. In the way of adrenalin, like she was
a sword still ringing from the first blow of what was going to be a
fight to the death.

"I love you," she said.

"I love you, too."

Was Floss even capable of love? Shit, that sounds hard. Makes
me a Grendel. But that was what I was thinking when she said it.
I guess I was pissed off about being left so entirely out of the loop.
And maybe I was hurting because she didn't try to persuade me
to stay.

All I got from MiCS was a curt nod. I was never a player for him, not a person of any consequence. As usual, he was busy scanning the room to see who was there and how they could be played and how he could milk this fiasco.

Soon a tide of well-wishers enveloped us and I found myself pushed to the margins.

I was never one for the big goodbye.

I decided not to go back to Dublin that night. I had my passport and ticket with me. I had my wallet. I only had one bag of clothes back in Bachelor's Quay, and it wasn't even worth the hassle to pick through them to check the pockets for illegal substances. Three strikes you're out—enough said. I borrowed an outfit from Marcel: white jeans (WTF?), a t-shirt with an image of Picasso holding a kitten, red socks, and tan boat shoes with tassels. Tommy Hilfiger move over.

So I took a cab straight to the airport, where I washed my hair in the bathroom sink. I bought a shamrock hoodie in a gift shop, then slept for a few hours on a bench. US Immigration seemed to find it suspicious that I had no check-in bags and no carry-on. Would they have looked the same way at some white businessman?—you can bet your ass they would not. When they did that hand-swab thing to me, the bleach residue must've set off the scanner alarm. So they insisted on a pat-down and a sniff-over from a sweet-looking beagle.

Finally, they let me board.

Up, up, and away. In-transit felt like freedom. Always did. I pictured being a kid and running along New Dorp beach, clipping off the ferny heads of seaside grasses with my wooden machete. And later, tired, lying back in the dunes while dragonflies hovered like drones above me. I fell asleep only to be awakened by the feeling I was being pulled up into the sky by the kite string I'd attached to my foot. It must have been the take-off. It must have been the butchered deer from the night before.

I refused headphones.

I refused newspapers, snacks, and drinks.

I refused to speak to the person next to me: a foxy, plus-size gal in a print dress who seemed interested. Though I did spend a while with my eyes closed, inhaling her sweet perfume, and thinking about cuddling her, being enfolded in all those folds of softness, kindness.

I reclined in my seat and looked look down on the pill-bottle, cotton-wool clouds.

Strangely, as I sat there in my chair in the sky, it wasn't flash-backs from the night before that played out before me. Nope. It was memories and images from our days together on the Camino. I only had to close my eyes and I could feel the bike under me. I could see the beige earth, the red roof tiles, the wide-open vistas of the Meseta. I could smell the dank bunkhouses of the *albergues*, the mineral smell of the old stone structures, the crypt-like coolness of the churches when you entered them at midday. I could see the smiles of the pilgrims as they set out in the morning. I recalled the disappointment on their faces as they wandered around in the courtyard outside the Santiago de Com-postela cathedral.

I had been changed by the experience, but in ways I didn't quite understand. All I knew was that I was slam-dunk-finito-finished with the art world.

Budsy's performance confirmed it.

The previous night was a flickering nightmare, a charnel house, a hag dream where you're paralyzed and suffocating and trying to wake up but you can't.

The art world was a horror. I pictured rooms filled with the living dead, those whose only interest in you was to find out what you thought about them. Whether you would add to or under-mine their brand. That's all they really wanted to know.

How had it come to be that this necessary, decent, human impulse—to create—a drive as deep as any appetite, had been twisted into some gross parody, turned inside-out to make some parallel universe, some maze? And once inside that maze, all your instincts for reinvention and renewal are perverted and rendered useless. It was strictly commercial.

The rat will choose cocaine over water. The rat will choose cocaine over food.

In my mind I heard the sound of a sheep bleating.

In my mind I heard a bone saw.

I didn't want to stand back and observe the world. I wanted to walk in the streets again and be at least on nodding acquaintance with my neighbours; to work in an ordinary job, coming home at the end of the day tired but not wired; to use my body, work with my hands making chairs, hats, rock walls—whatever—frame houses, push a mop and pail, earbuds playing Mozart. I wanted to ac/dc with other human beings. Behold the living face, not the portrait of the face.

I kept picturing a country garden, bees humming in the flowering hedges and the breeze conjuring an ocean in the leaves of poplar trees, while I swept a scythe through an acre of grass, that motion anchoring me in my body.

Afterwards, sitting down to a simple supper: the taste of green onion, beets, trout fried in butter. Washing it down with a glass of lukewarm water.

Later again, in my Adirondack chair, smoking a doob and listening to the woodpecker strike through me; marvelling at the wasps' nest, how those hated papermakers build a labyrinth.

Then, in darkness, lying face-to-face with my sleeping lover, smell of anise on her breath.

I wanted the earth under my feet, the sky above, the trees, the rivers, and the mountains in between—I didn't want my experience to be mediated.

I was done with being the Apostle J. I wanted to live exposed, not protected. I wanted to live like I'd been living when I first became friends with Floss and Budsy.

For a while, our aims were true.

What we pursued seemed to be worth the price.

But all that had soured, and my friends seemed to be disappearing forever inside the funhouse.

Never say forever.

Maybe they would be strong enough to walk away from the mirrored maze.

Maybe they would find a way to bend it to their will.

To fulfill and be fulfilled.

Never say.